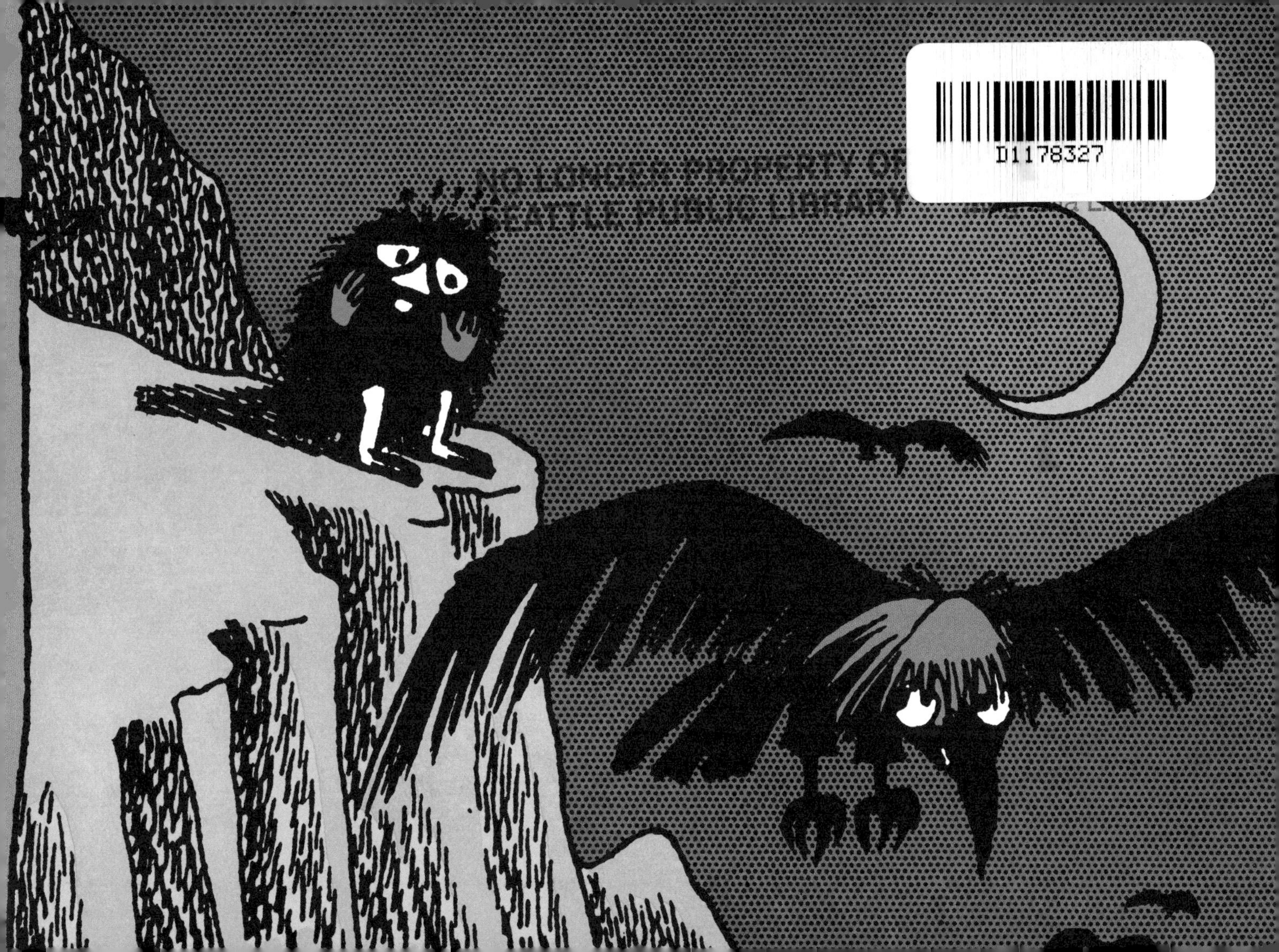

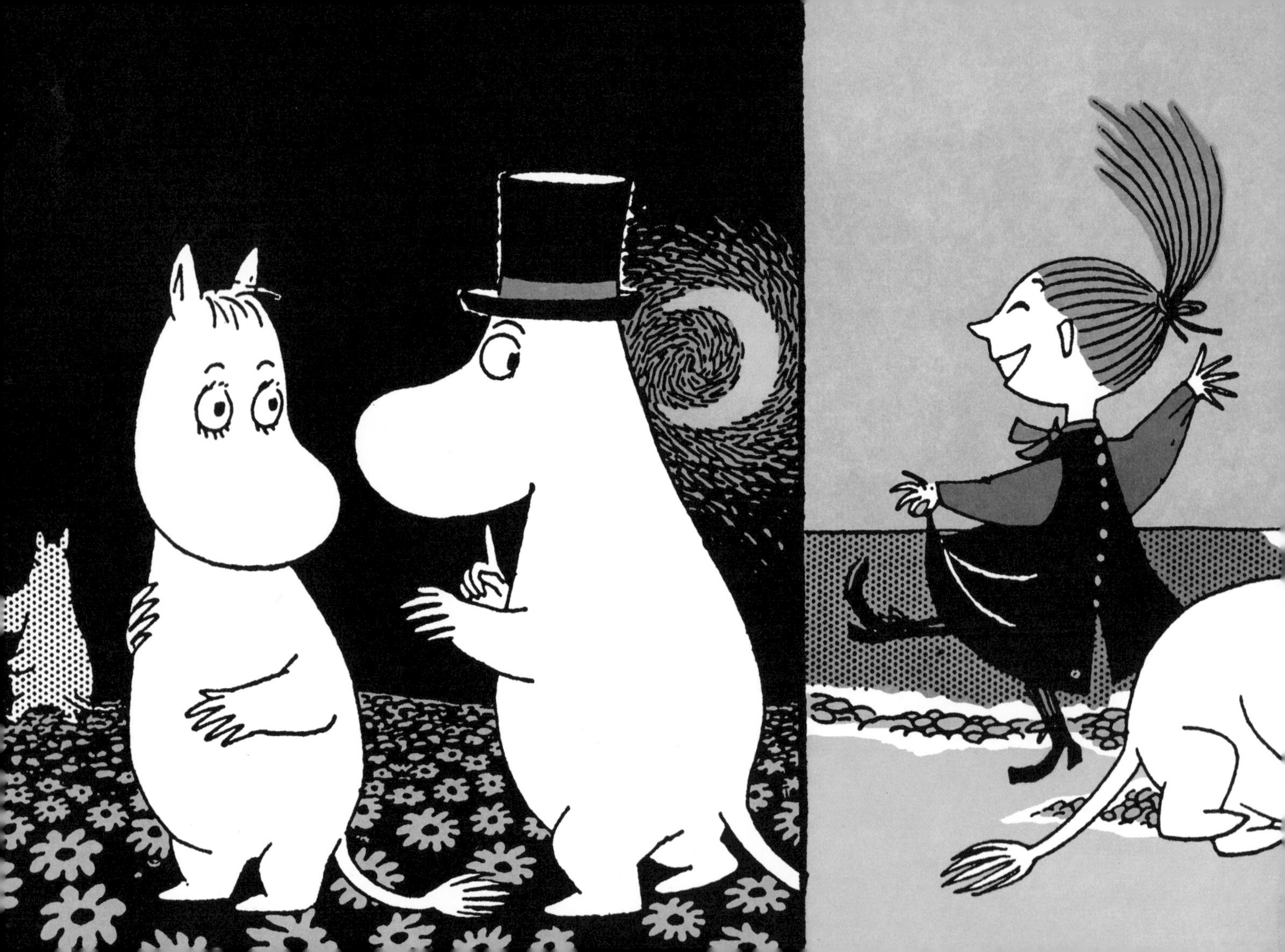

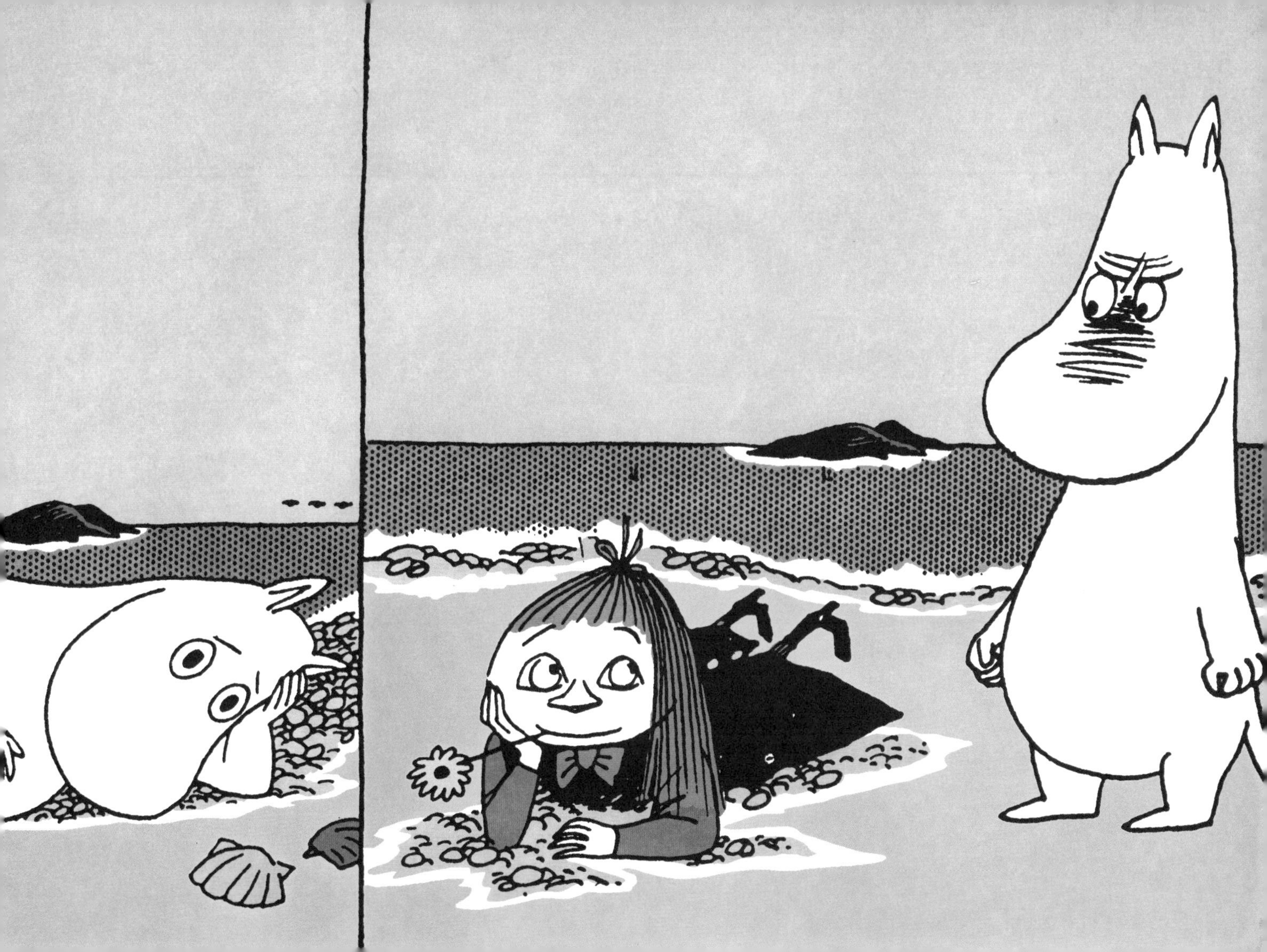

drawnandquarterly.com
First edition: July 2017
Printed in Malaysia
10 9 8 7 6 5 4 3 2 1

Library and Archives Canada Cataloguing in Publication
Jansson, Tove, author, illustrator
Moomin Begins a New Life / Tove Jansson.
ISBN 978-1-77046-271-7 (paperback)
1. Comics (Graphic works). I. Jansson, Tove. Moomin. II. Title.
PZ7.7.J35MOBE 2017 J741.5'94897 C2016-904685-0

Published in the USA by Drawn & Quarterly, a client publisher of Farrar, Straus and Giroux. Orders: 888.330.8477

Published in Canada by Drawn & Quarterly, a client publisher of Raincoast Books. Orders: 800.663.5714

Published in the United Kingdom by Drawn & Quarterly, a client publisher of Publishers Group UK. Orders: info@pguk.co.uk

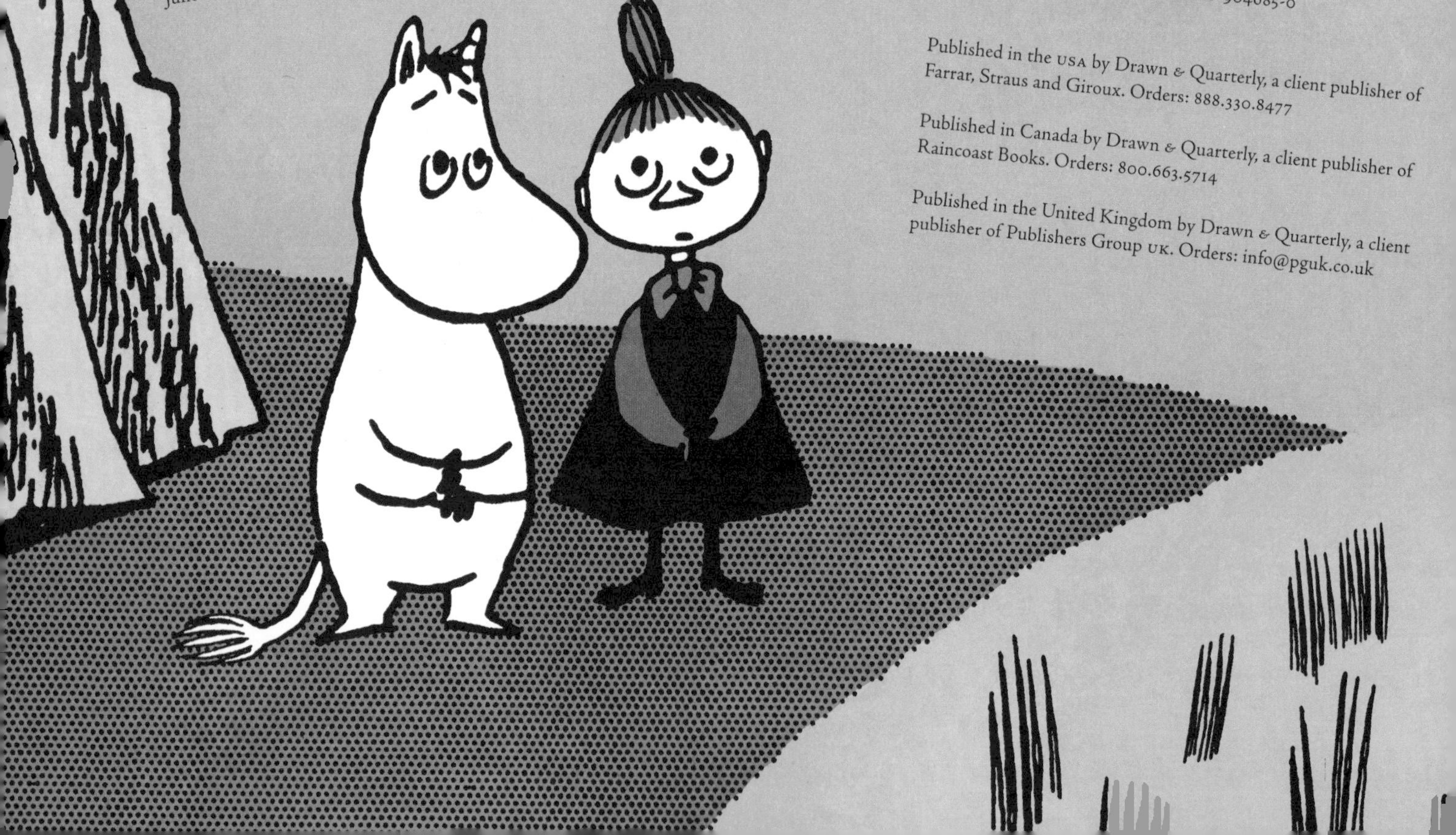

MOOMIN BEGINS A NEW LIFE

Tove Jansson

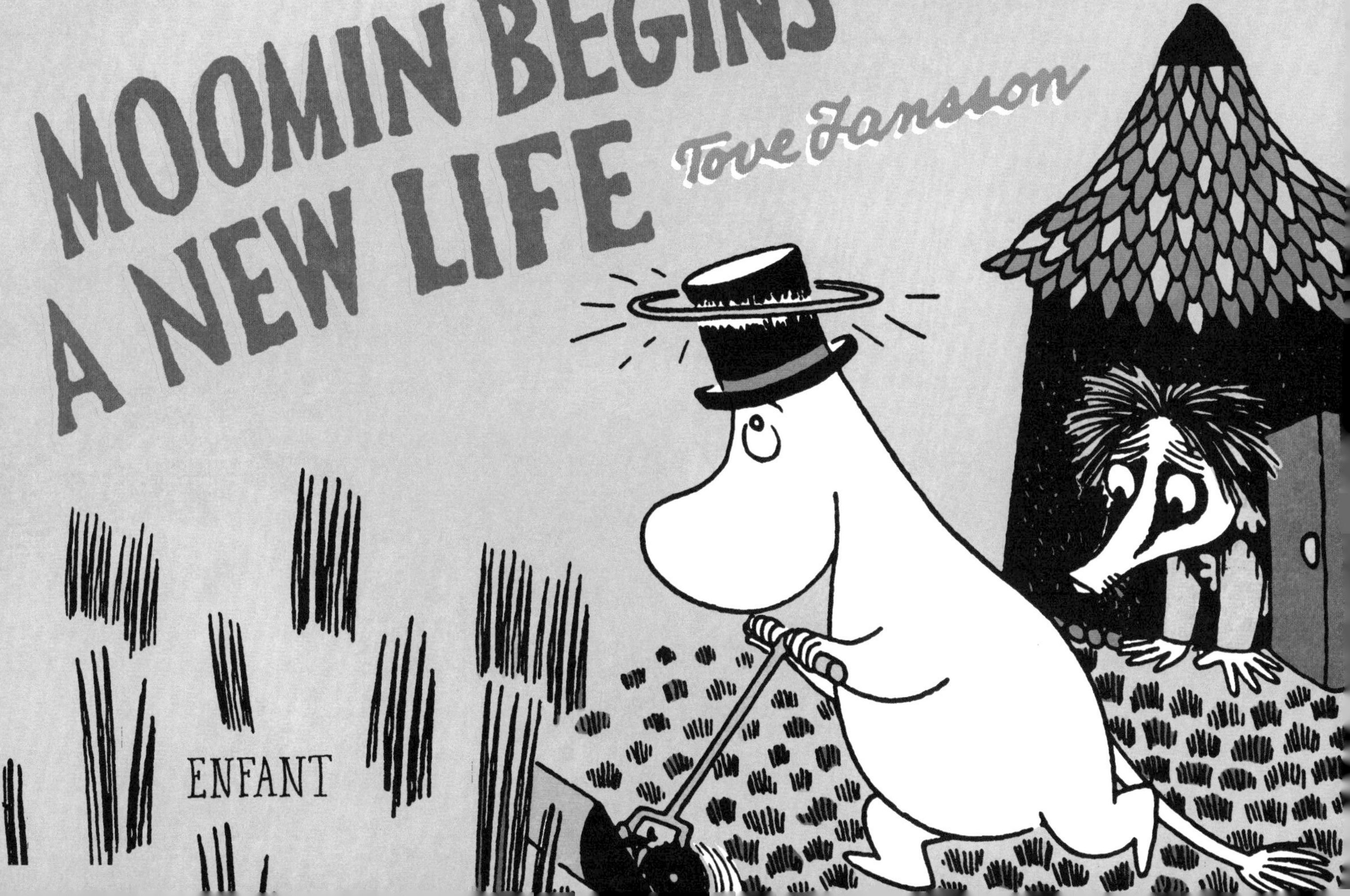

ENFANT

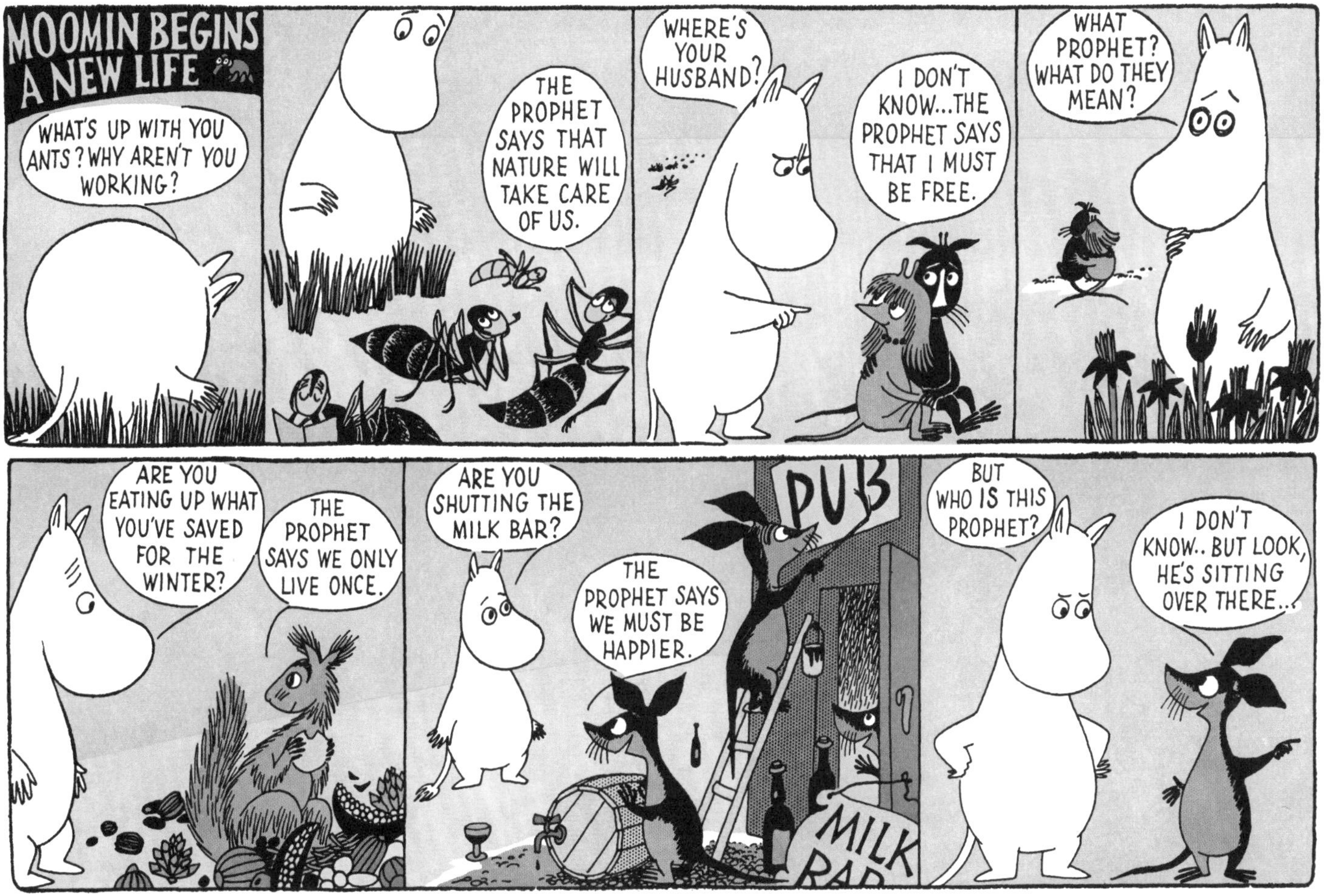
MOOMIN BEGINS A NEW LIFE
WHAT'S UP WITH YOU ANTS? WHY AREN'T YOU WORKING?
THE PROPHET SAYS THAT NATURE WILL TAKE CARE OF US.
WHERE'S YOUR HUSBAND?
I DON'T KNOW...THE PROPHET SAYS THAT I MUST BE FREE.
WHAT PROPHET? WHAT DO THEY MEAN?
ARE YOU EATING UP WHAT YOU'VE SAVED FOR THE WINTER?
THE PROPHET SAYS WE ONLY LIVE ONCE.
ARE YOU SHUTTING THE MILK BAR?
THE PROPHET SAYS WE MUST BE HAPPIER.
PUB
MILK BAR
BUT WHO IS THIS PROPHET?
I DON'T KNOW.. BUT LOOK, HE'S SITTING OVER THERE...

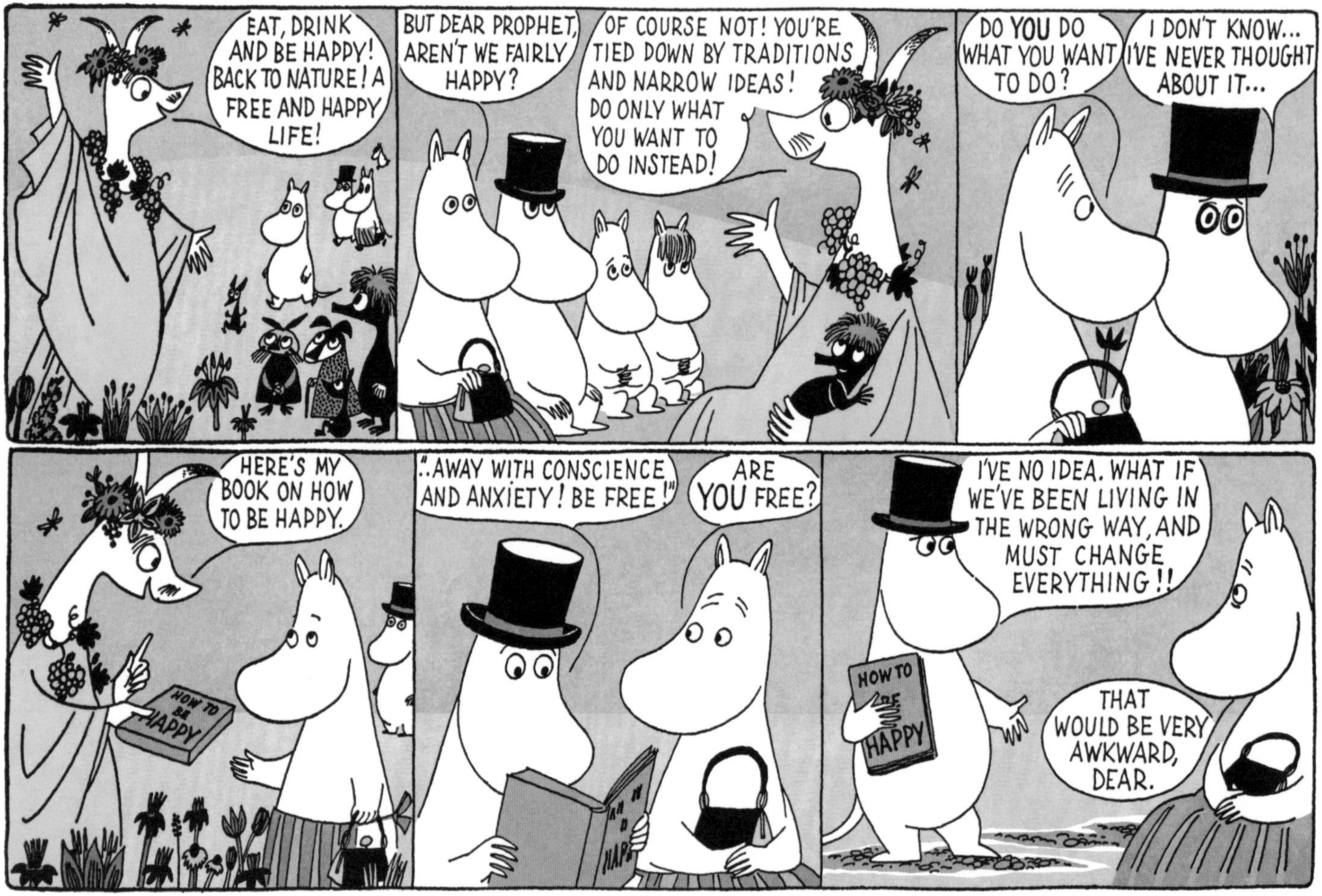
EAT, DRINK AND BE HAPPY! BACK TO NATURE! A FREE AND HAPPY LIFE!
BUT DEAR PROPHET, AREN'T WE FAIRLY HAPPY?
OF COURSE NOT! YOU'RE TIED DOWN BY TRADITIONS AND NARROW IDEAS! DO ONLY WHAT YOU WANT TO DO INSTEAD!
DO YOU DO WHAT YOU WANT TO DO?
I DON'T KNOW... I'VE NEVER THOUGHT ABOUT IT...
HERE'S MY BOOK ON HOW TO BE HAPPY.
HOW TO BE HAPPY
"..AWAY WITH CONSCIENCE AND ANXIETY! BE FREE!"
ARE YOU FREE?
I'VE NO IDEA. WHAT IF WE'VE BEEN LIVING IN THE WRONG WAY, AND MUST CHANGE EVERYTHING!!
HOW TO BE HAPPY
THAT WOULD BE VERY AWKWARD, DEAR.

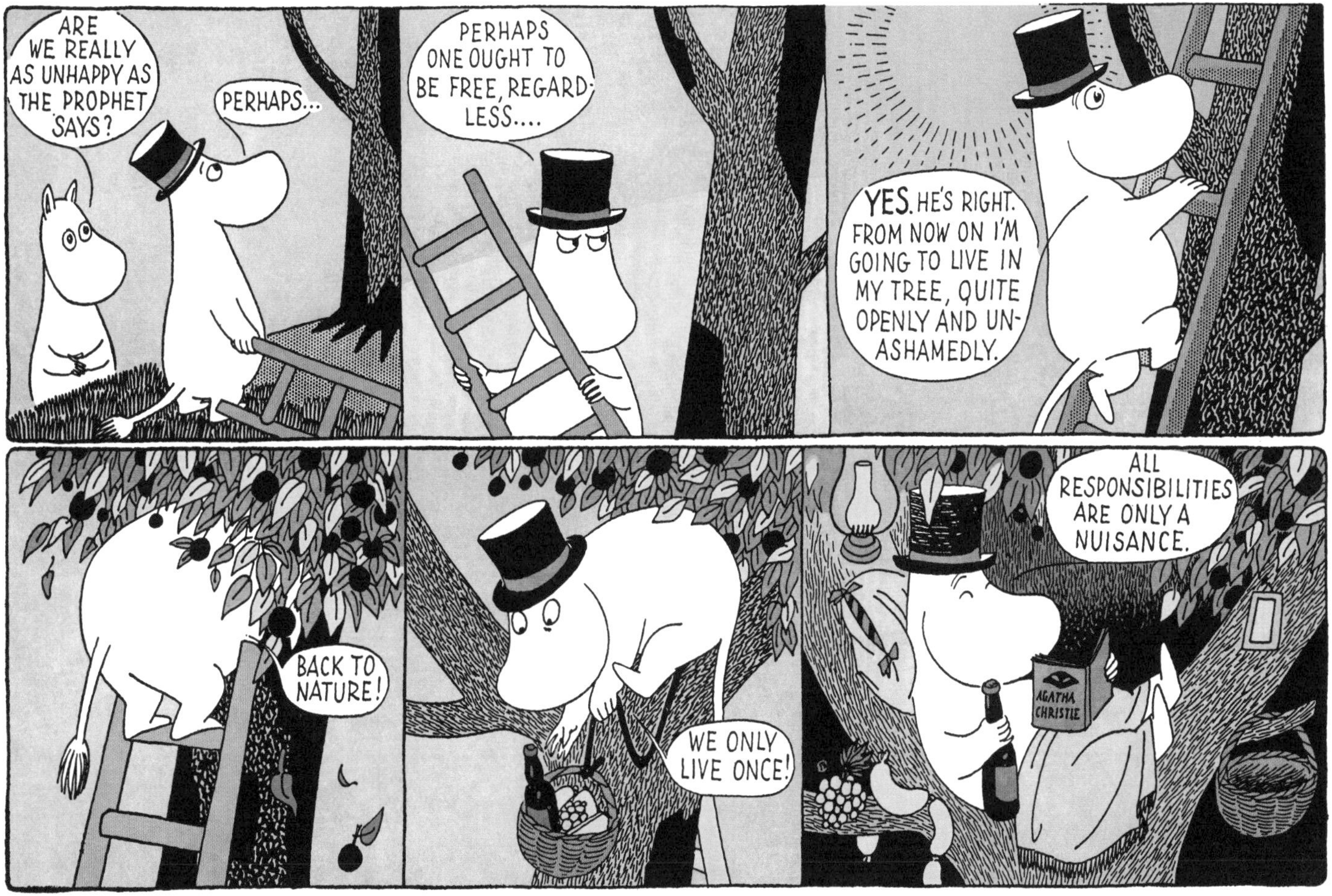
ARE WE REALLY AS UNHAPPY AS THE PROPHET SAYS?
PERHAPS...
PERHAPS ONE OUGHT TO BE FREE, REGARD-LESS....
YES. HE'S RIGHT. FROM NOW ON I'M GOING TO LIVE IN MY TREE, QUITE OPENLY AND UN-ASHAMEDLY.
BACK TO NATURE!
WE ONLY LIVE ONCE!
ALL RESPONSIBILITIES ARE ONLY A NUISANCE.
AGATHA CHRISTIE

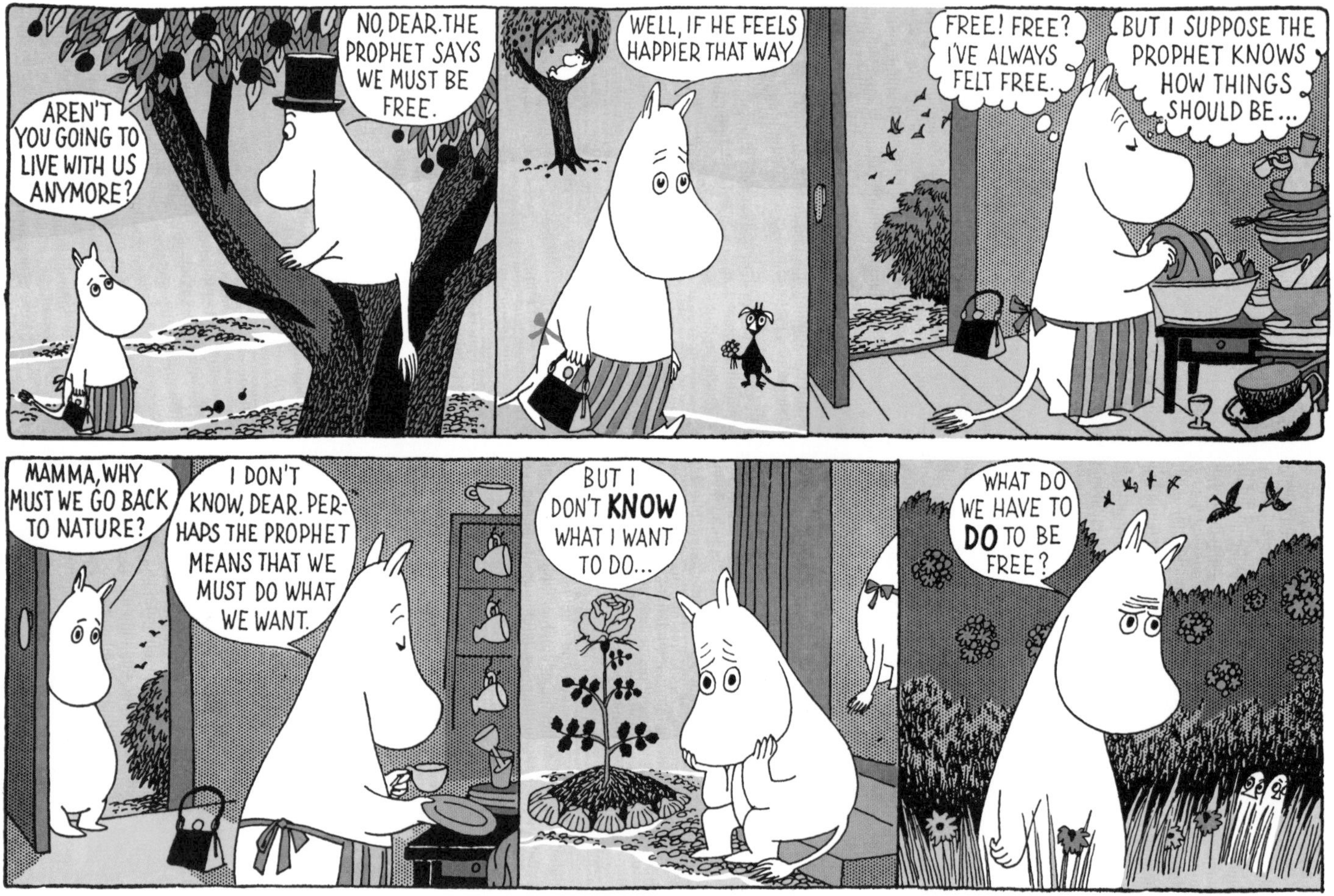
AREN'T YOU GOING TO LIVE WITH US ANYMORE?
NO, DEAR. THE PROPHET SAYS WE MUST BE FREE.
WELL, IF HE FEELS HAPPIER THAT WAY
FREE! FREE? I'VE ALWAYS FELT FREE.
BUT I SUPPOSE THE PROPHET KNOWS HOW THINGS SHOULD BE...
MAMMA, WHY MUST WE GO BACK TO NATURE?
I DON'T KNOW, DEAR. PERHAPS THE PROPHET MEANS THAT WE MUST DO WHAT WE WANT.
BUT I DON'T **KNOW** WHAT I WANT TO DO...
WHAT DO WE HAVE TO **DO** TO BE FREE?

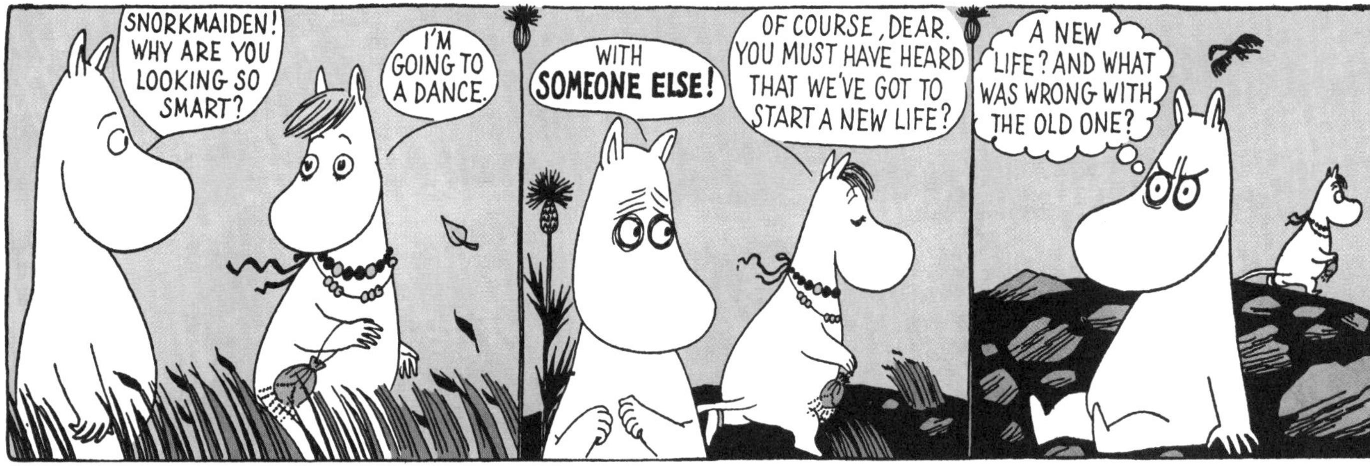
SNORKMAIDEN! WHY ARE YOU LOOKING SO SMART?
I'M GOING TO A DANCE.
WITH **SOMEONE ELSE!**
OF COURSE, DEAR. YOU MUST HAVE HEARD THAT WE'VE GOT TO START A NEW LIFE?
A NEW LIFE? AND WHAT WAS WRONG WITH THE OLD ONE?

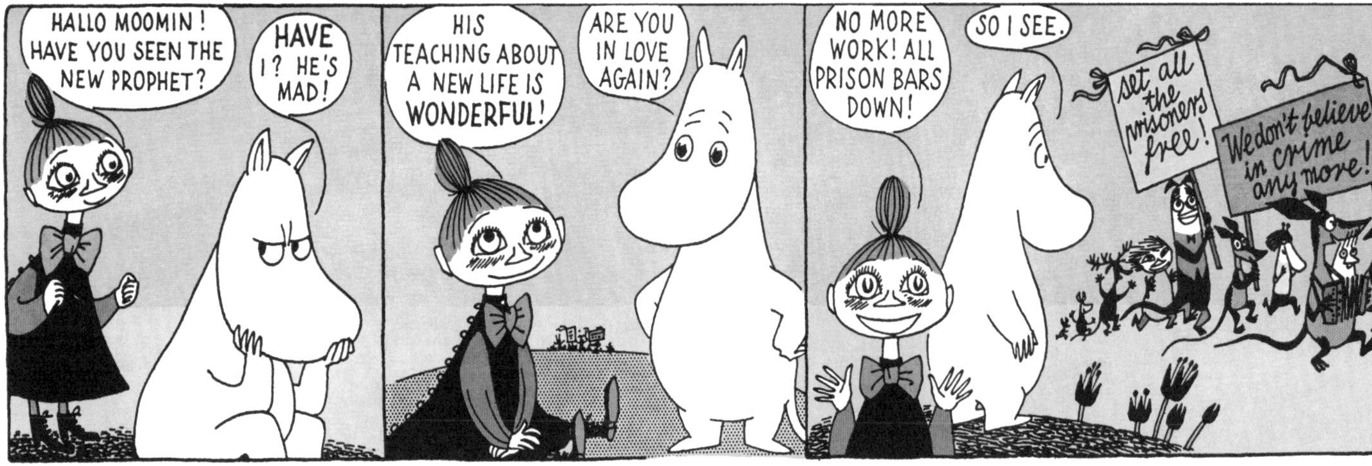
HALLO MOOMIN! HAVE YOU SEEN THE NEW PROPHET?
HAVE I? HE'S MAD!
HIS TEACHING ABOUT A NEW LIFE IS **WONDERFUL!**
ARE YOU IN LOVE AGAIN?
NO MORE WORK! ALL PRISON BARS DOWN!
SO I SEE.
set all the prisoners free!
We don't believe in crime any more!

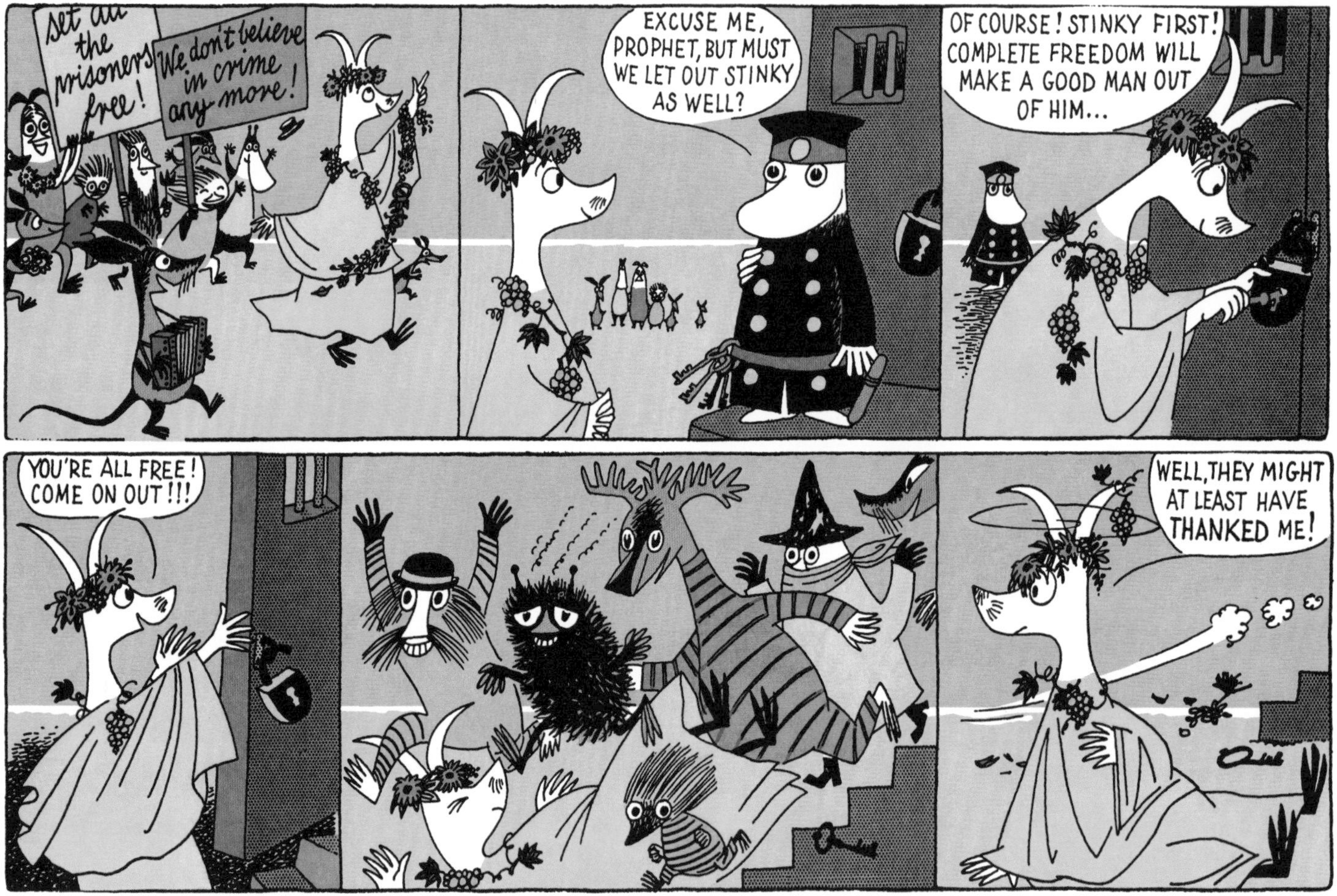
Set all the prisoners free!
We don't believe in crime any more!
EXCUSE ME, PROPHET, BUT MUST WE LET OUT STINKY AS WELL?
OF COURSE! STINKY FIRST! COMPLETE FREEDOM WILL MAKE A GOOD MAN OUT OF HIM...
YOU'RE ALL FREE! COME ON OUT!!!
WELL, THEY MIGHT AT LEAST HAVE THANKED ME!

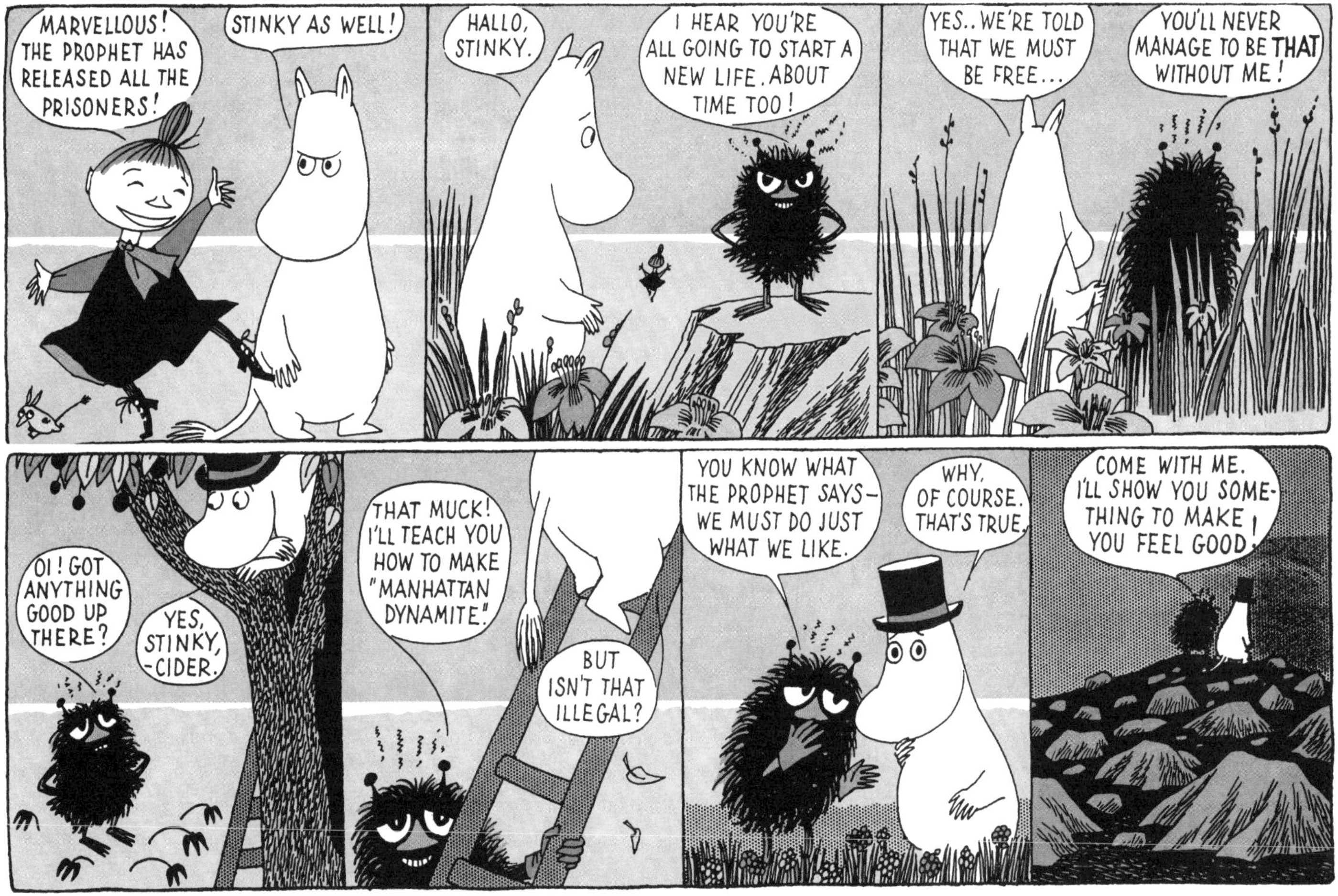
MARVELLOUS! THE PROPHET HAS RELEASED ALL THE PRISONERS!
STINKY AS WELL!
HALLO, STINKY.
I HEAR YOU'RE ALL GOING TO START A NEW LIFE. ABOUT TIME TOO!
YES.. WE'RE TOLD THAT WE MUST BE FREE...
YOU'LL NEVER MANAGE TO BE THAT WITHOUT ME!
OI! GOT ANYTHING GOOD UP THERE?
YES, STINKY, -CIDER.
THAT MUCK! I'LL TEACH YOU HOW TO MAKE "MANHATTAN DYNAMITE."
BUT ISN'T THAT ILLEGAL?
YOU KNOW WHAT THE PROPHET SAYS — WE MUST DO JUST WHAT WE LIKE.
WHY, OF COURSE. THAT'S TRUE.
COME WITH ME. I'LL SHOW YOU SOMETHING TO MAKE YOU FEEL GOOD!

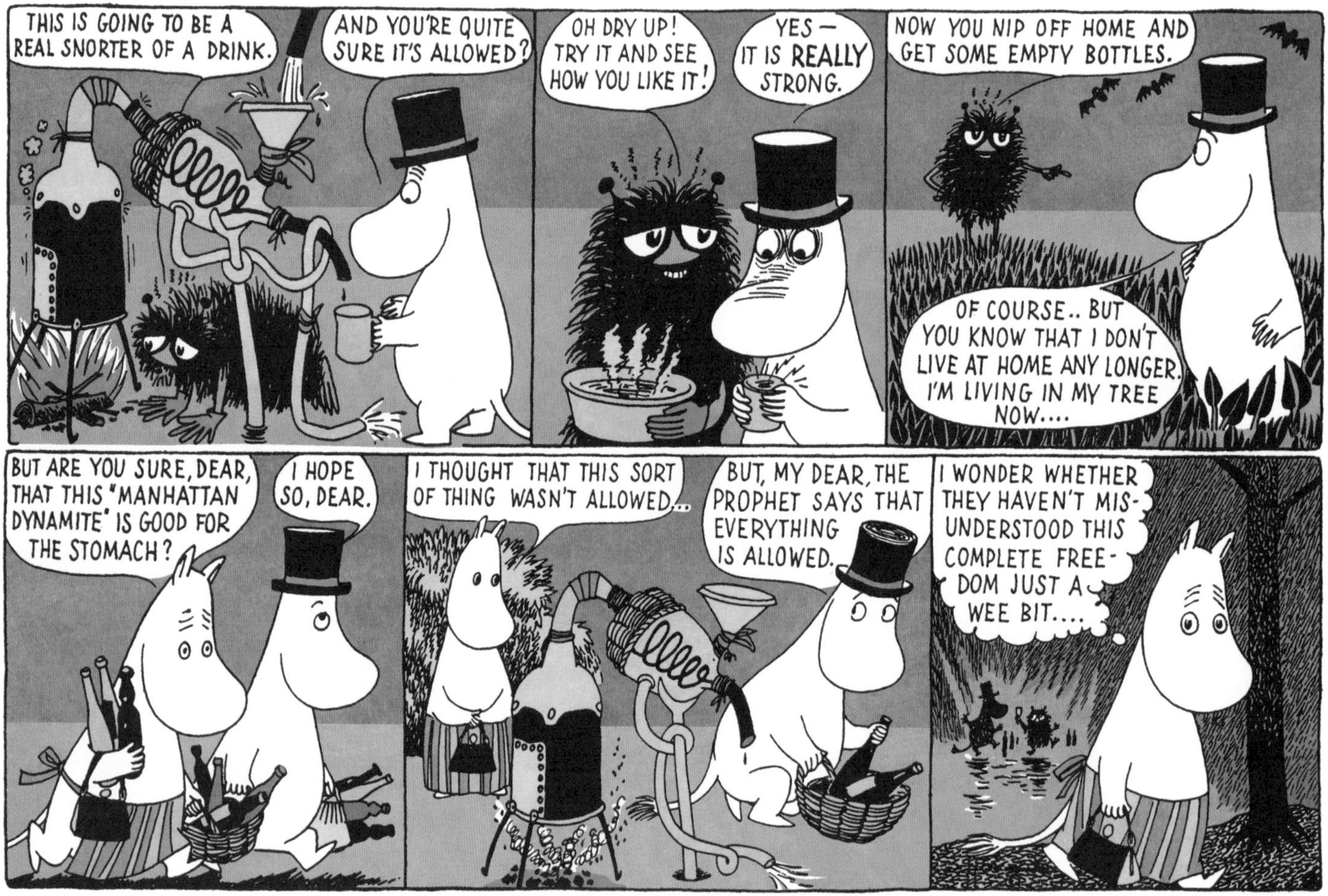
THIS IS GOING TO BE A REAL SNORTER OF A DRINK.
AND YOU'RE QUITE SURE IT'S ALLOWED?
OH DRY UP! TRY IT AND SEE HOW YOU LIKE IT!
YES — IT IS REALLY STRONG.
NOW YOU NIP OFF HOME AND GET SOME EMPTY BOTTLES.
OF COURSE.. BUT YOU KNOW THAT I DON'T LIVE AT HOME ANY LONGER. I'M LIVING IN MY TREE NOW....
BUT ARE YOU SURE, DEAR, THAT THIS "MANHATTAN DYNAMITE" IS GOOD FOR THE STOMACH?
I HOPE SO, DEAR.
I THOUGHT THAT THIS SORT OF THING WASN'T ALLOWED...
BUT, MY DEAR, THE PROPHET SAYS THAT EVERYTHING IS ALLOWED.
I WONDER WHETHER THEY HAVEN'T MIS-UNDERSTOOD THIS COMPLETE FREE-DOM JUST A WEE BIT....

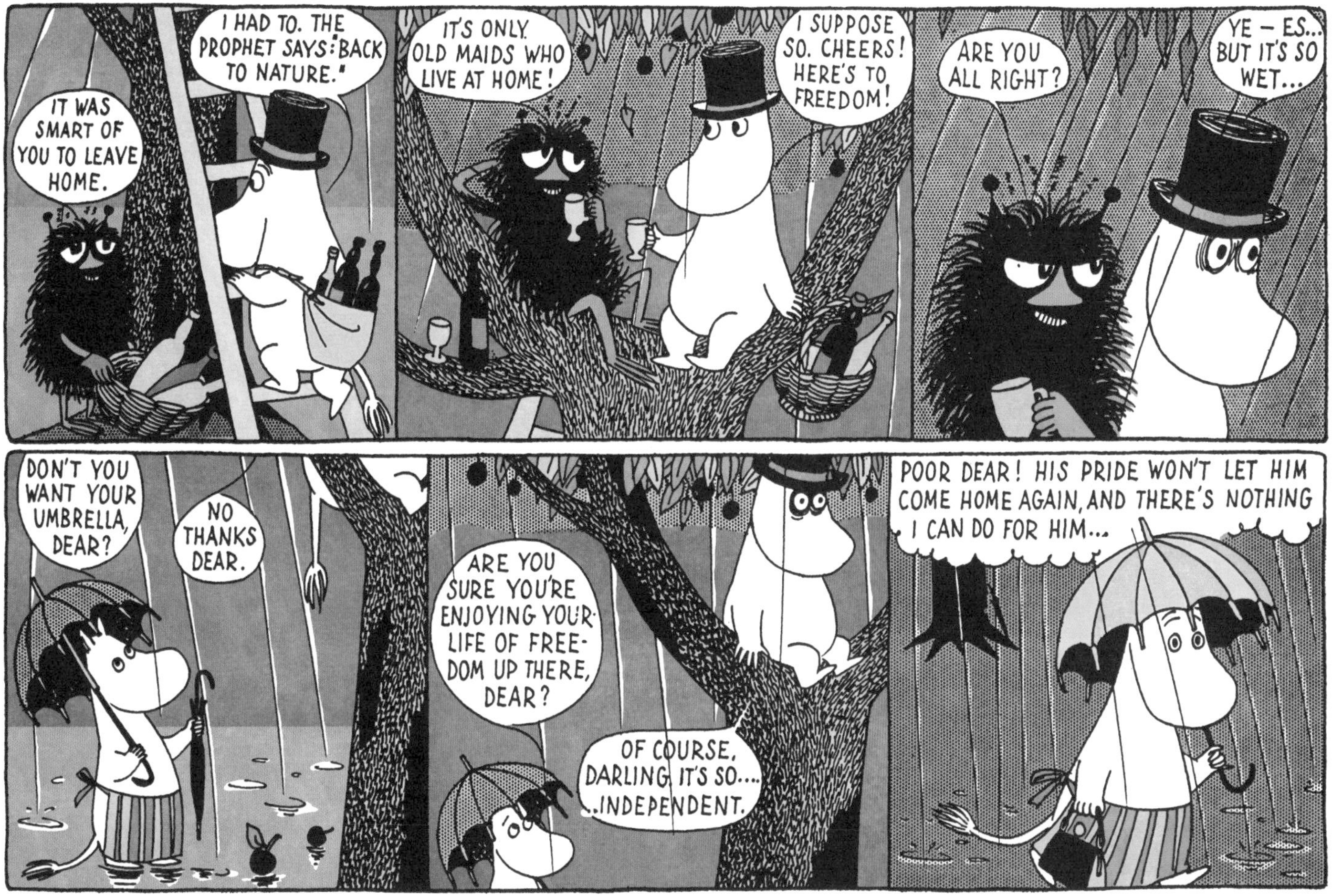
I HAD TO. THE PROPHET SAYS: "BACK TO NATURE."
IT WAS SMART OF YOU TO LEAVE HOME.
IT'S ONLY OLD MAIDS WHO LIVE AT HOME!
I SUPPOSE SO. CHEERS! HERE'S TO FREEDOM!
ARE YOU ALL RIGHT?
YE — ES... BUT IT'S SO WET...
DON'T YOU WANT YOUR UMBRELLA, DEAR?
NO THANKS DEAR.
ARE YOU SURE YOU'RE ENJOYING YOUR LIFE OF FREE-DOM UP THERE, DEAR?
OF COURSE, DARLING IT'S SO.... ..INDEPENDENT.
POOR DEAR! HIS PRIDE WON'T LET HIM COME HOME AGAIN, AND THERE'S NOTHING I CAN DO FOR HIM...

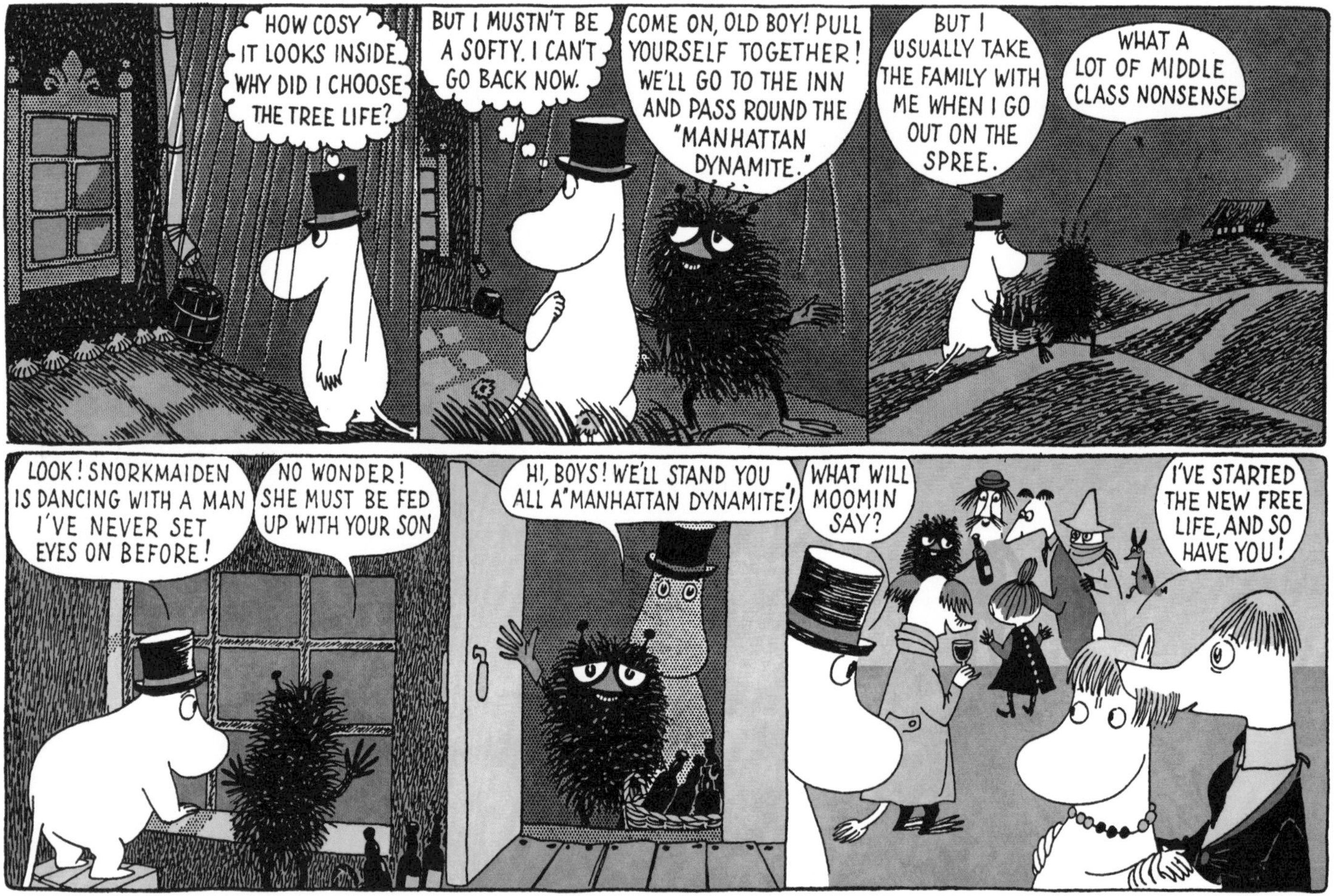
HOW COSY IT LOOKS INSIDE. WHY DID I CHOOSE THE TREE LIFE?
BUT I MUSTN'T BE A SOFTY. I CAN'T GO BACK NOW.
COME ON, OLD BOY! PULL YOURSELF TOGETHER! WE'LL GO TO THE INN AND PASS ROUND THE "MANHATTAN DYNAMITE."
BUT I USUALLY TAKE THE FAMILY WITH ME WHEN I GO OUT ON THE SPREE.
WHAT A LOT OF MIDDLE CLASS NONSENSE.
LOOK! SNORKMAIDEN IS DANCING WITH A MAN I'VE NEVER SET EYES ON BEFORE!
NO WONDER! SHE MUST BE FED UP WITH YOUR SON
HI, BOYS! WE'LL STAND YOU ALL A "MANHATTAN DYNAMITE"!
WHAT WILL MOOMIN SAY?
I'VE STARTED THE NEW FREE LIFE, AND SO HAVE YOU!

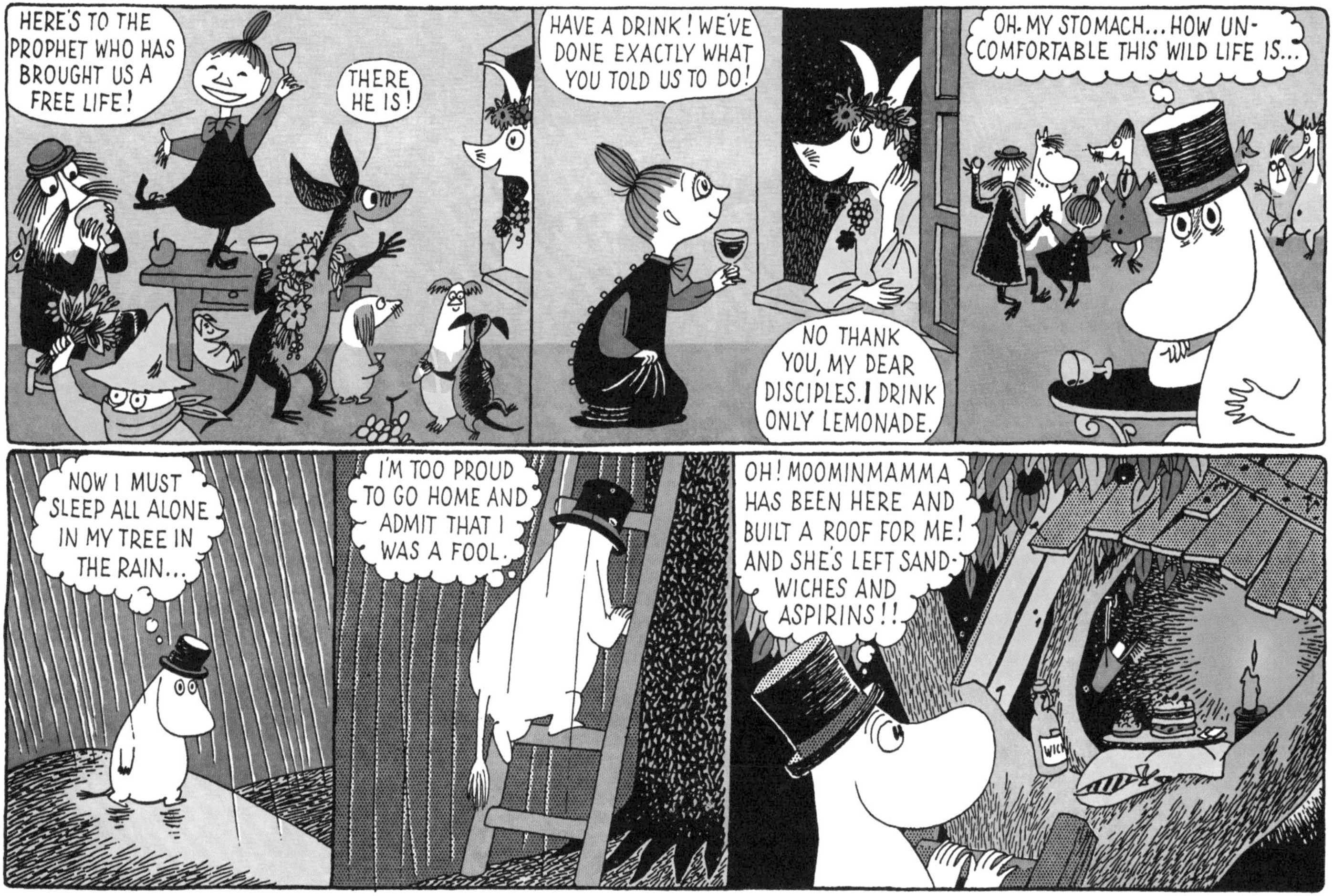

HERE'S TO THE PROPHET WHO HAS BROUGHT US A FREE LIFE!
THERE HE IS!
HAVE A DRINK! WE'VE DONE EXACTLY WHAT YOU TOLD US TO DO!
NO THANK YOU, MY DEAR DISCIPLES. I DRINK ONLY LEMONADE.
OH. MY STOMACH... HOW UN-COMFORTABLE THIS WILD LIFE IS...
NOW I MUST SLEEP ALL ALONE IN MY TREE IN THE RAIN...
I'M TOO PROUD TO GO HOME AND ADMIT THAT I WAS A FOOL.
OH! MOOMINMAMMA HAS BEEN HERE AND BUILT A ROOF FOR ME! AND SHE'S LEFT SAND-WICHES AND ASPIRINS!!

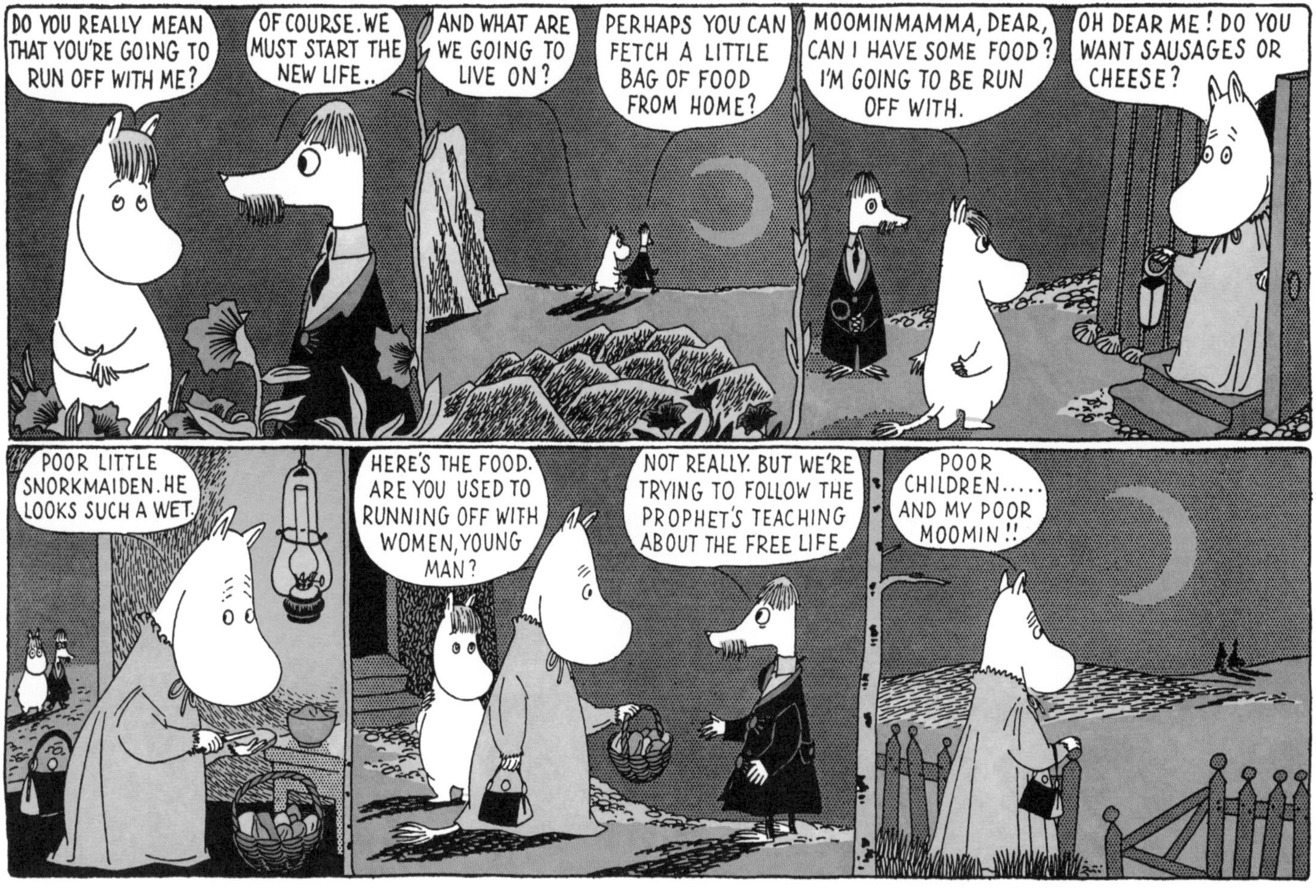
DO YOU REALLY MEAN THAT YOU'RE GOING TO RUN OFF WITH ME?
OF COURSE. WE MUST START THE NEW LIFE..
AND WHAT ARE WE GOING TO LIVE ON?
PERHAPS YOU CAN FETCH A LITTLE BAG OF FOOD FROM HOME?
MOOMINMAMMA, DEAR, CAN I HAVE SOME FOOD? I'M GOING TO BE RUN OFF WITH.
OH DEAR ME! DO YOU WANT SAUSAGES OR CHEESE?
POOR LITTLE SNORKMAIDEN. HE LOOKS SUCH A WET.
HERE'S THE FOOD. ARE YOU USED TO RUNNING OFF WITH WOMEN, YOUNG MAN?
NOT REALLY. BUT WE'RE TRYING TO FOLLOW THE PROPHET'S TEACHING ABOUT THE FREE LIFE.
POOR CHILDREN..... AND MY POOR MOOMIN!!

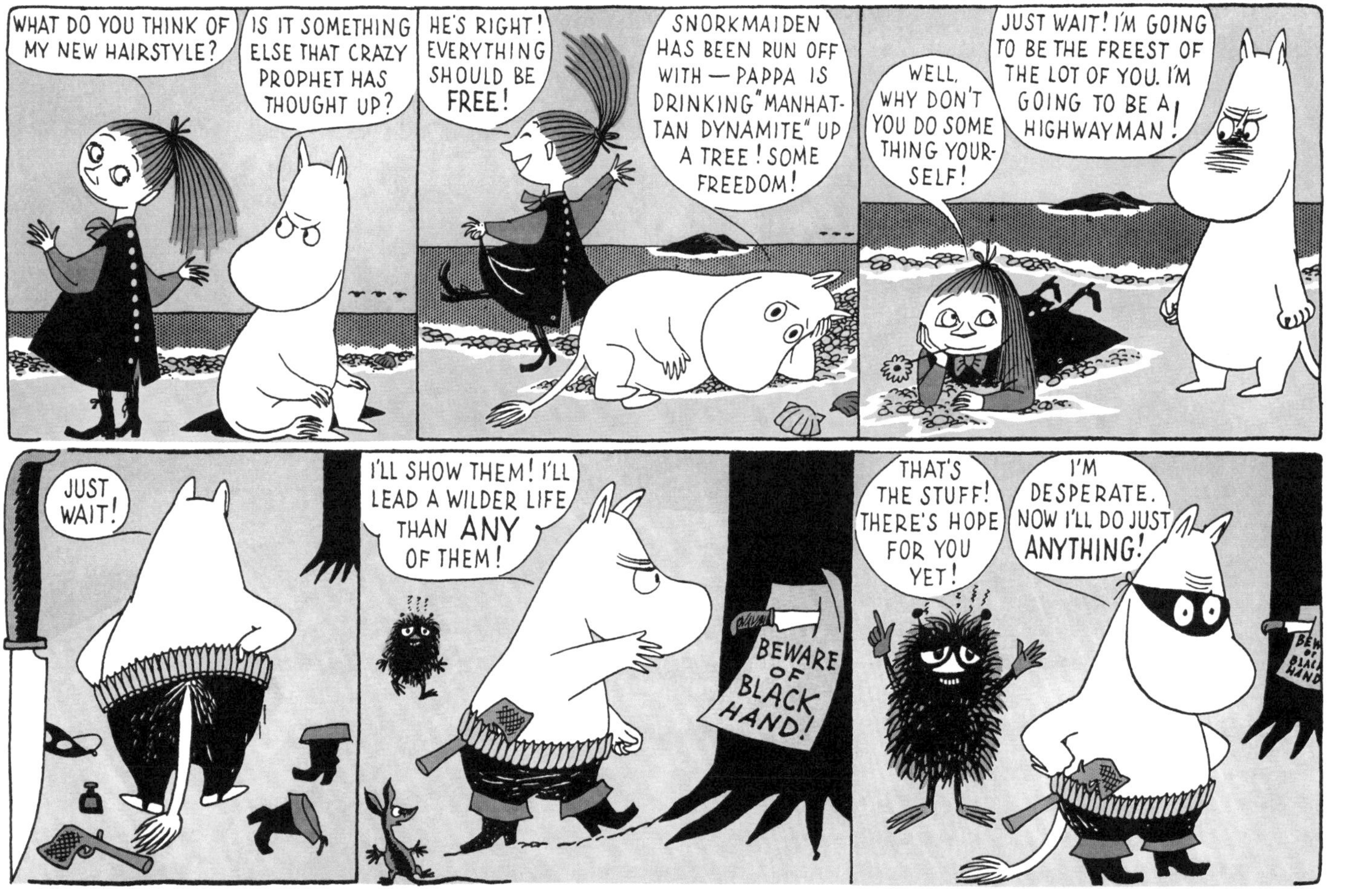
WHAT DO YOU THINK OF MY NEW HAIRSTYLE?
IS IT SOMETHING ELSE THAT CRAZY PROPHET HAS THOUGHT UP?
HE'S RIGHT! EVERYTHING SHOULD BE FREE!
SNORKMAIDEN HAS BEEN RUN OFF WITH — PAPPA IS DRINKING "MANHATTAN DYNAMITE" UP A TREE! SOME FREEDOM!
WELL, WHY DON'T YOU DO SOME THING YOURSELF!
JUST WAIT! I'M GOING TO BE THE FREEST OF THE LOT OF YOU. I'M GOING TO BE A HIGHWAYMAN!
JUST WAIT!
I'LL SHOW THEM! I'LL LEAD A WILDER LIFE THAN ANY OF THEM!
BEWARE OF BLACK HAND!
THAT'S THE STUFF! THERE'S HOPE FOR YOU YET!
I'M DESPERATE. NOW I'LL DO JUST ANYTHING!

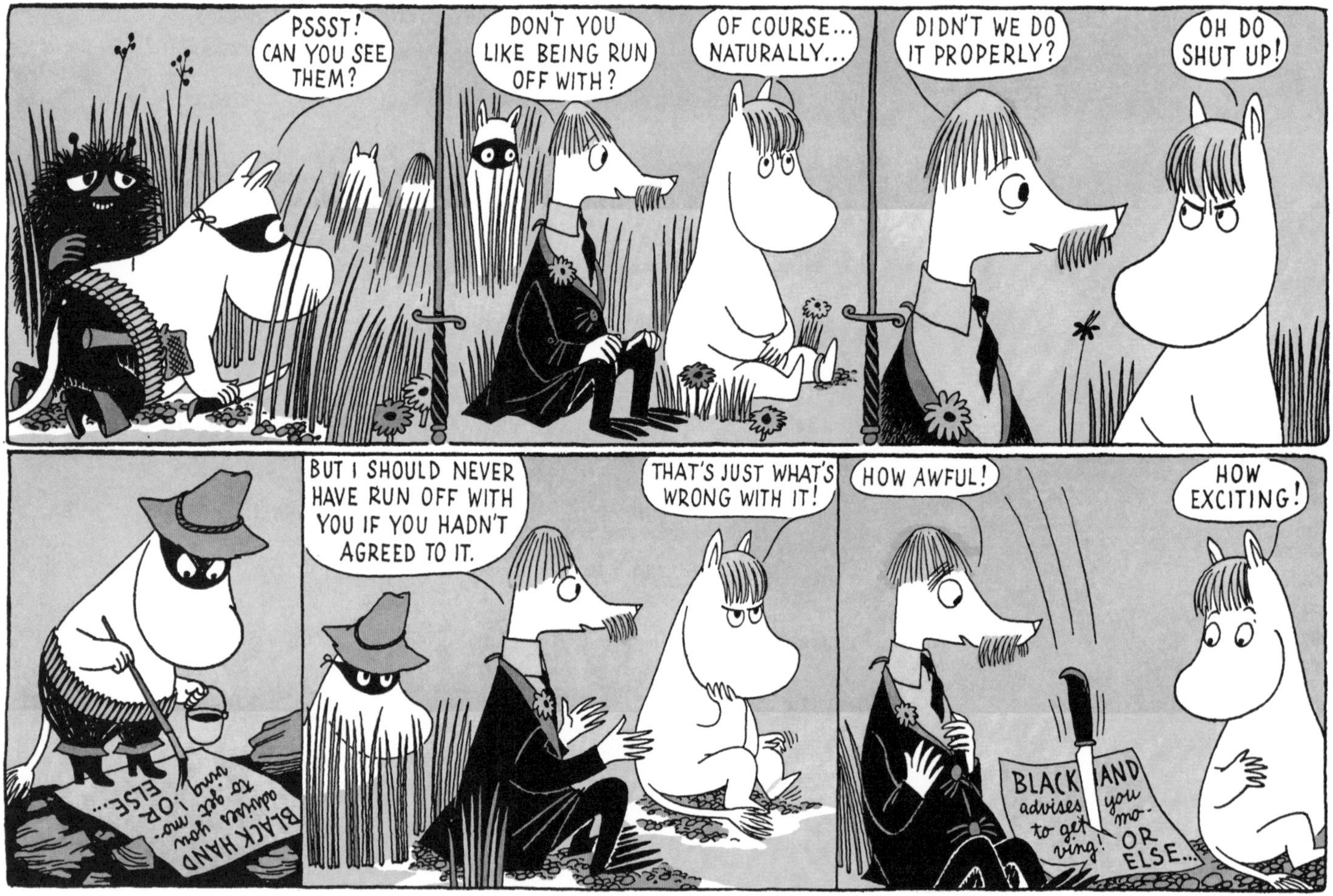
PSSST! CAN YOU SEE THEM?
DON'T YOU LIKE BEING RUN OFF WITH?
OF COURSE... NATURALLY...
DIDN'T WE DO IT PROPERLY?
OH DO SHUT UP!
BLACK HAND advises you to get mo- ving! OR ELSE...
BUT I SHOULD NEVER HAVE RUN OFF WITH YOU IF YOU HADN'T AGREED TO IT.
THAT'S JUST WHAT'S WRONG WITH IT!
HOW AWFUL!
HOW EXCITING!
BLACK
AND
advises you
to get mo-
ving! OR
ELSE...

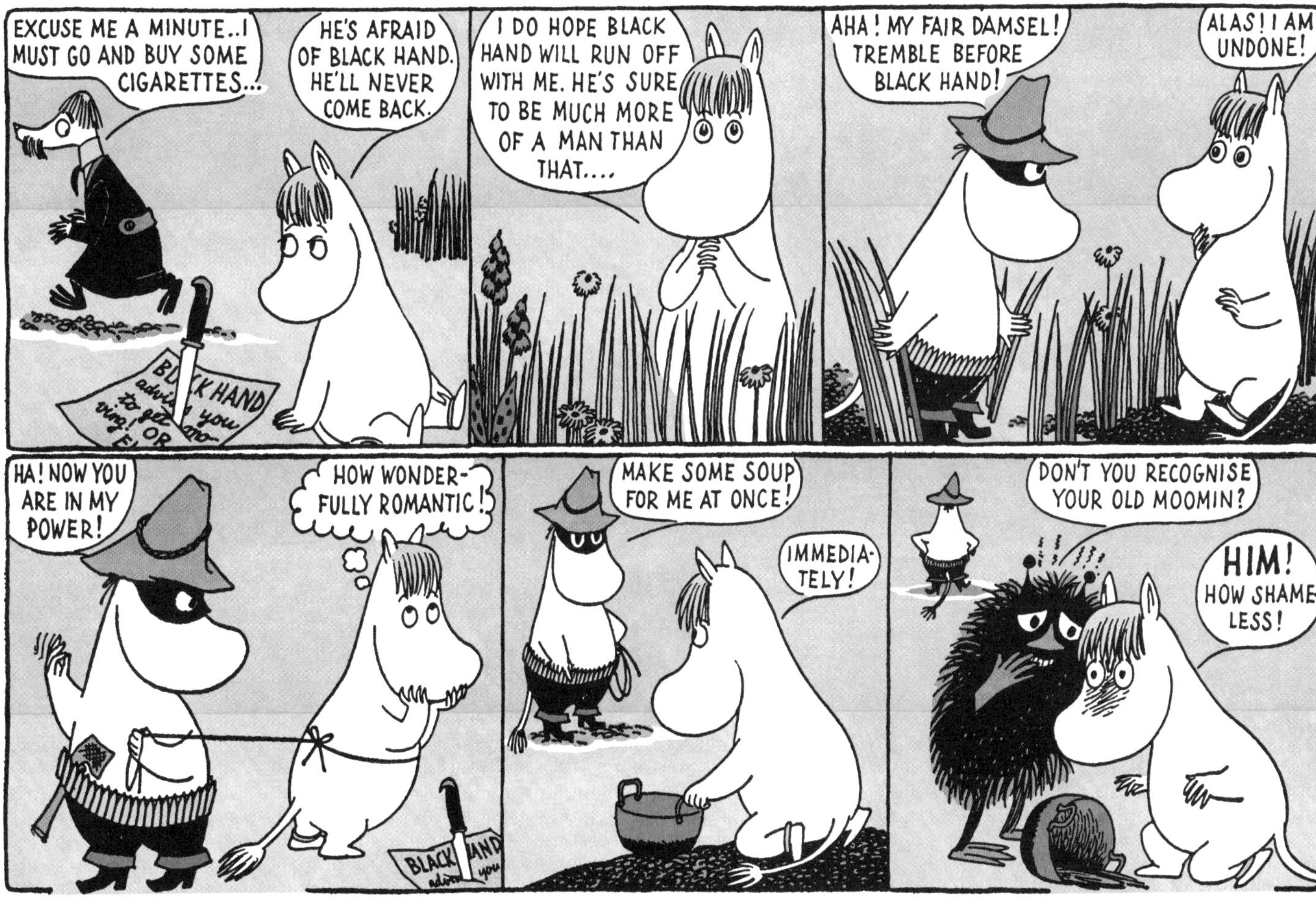
EXCUSE ME A MINUTE..I MUST GO AND BUY SOME CIGARETTES...
HE'S AFRAID OF BLACK HAND. HE'LL NEVER COME BACK.
BLACK HAND advises you to get mo- ving! OR
I DO HOPE BLACK HAND WILL RUN OFF WITH ME. HE'S SURE TO BE MUCH MORE OF A MAN THAN THAT....
AHA! MY FAIR DAMSEL! TREMBLE BEFORE BLACK HAND!
ALAS! I AM UNDONE!
HA! NOW YOU ARE IN MY POWER!
HOW WONDER-FULLY ROMANTIC!
BLACK HAND advises you
MAKE SOME SOUP FOR ME AT ONCE!
IMMEDIA-TELY!
DON'T YOU RECOGNISE YOUR OLD MOOMIN?
HIM! HOW SHAME-LESS!

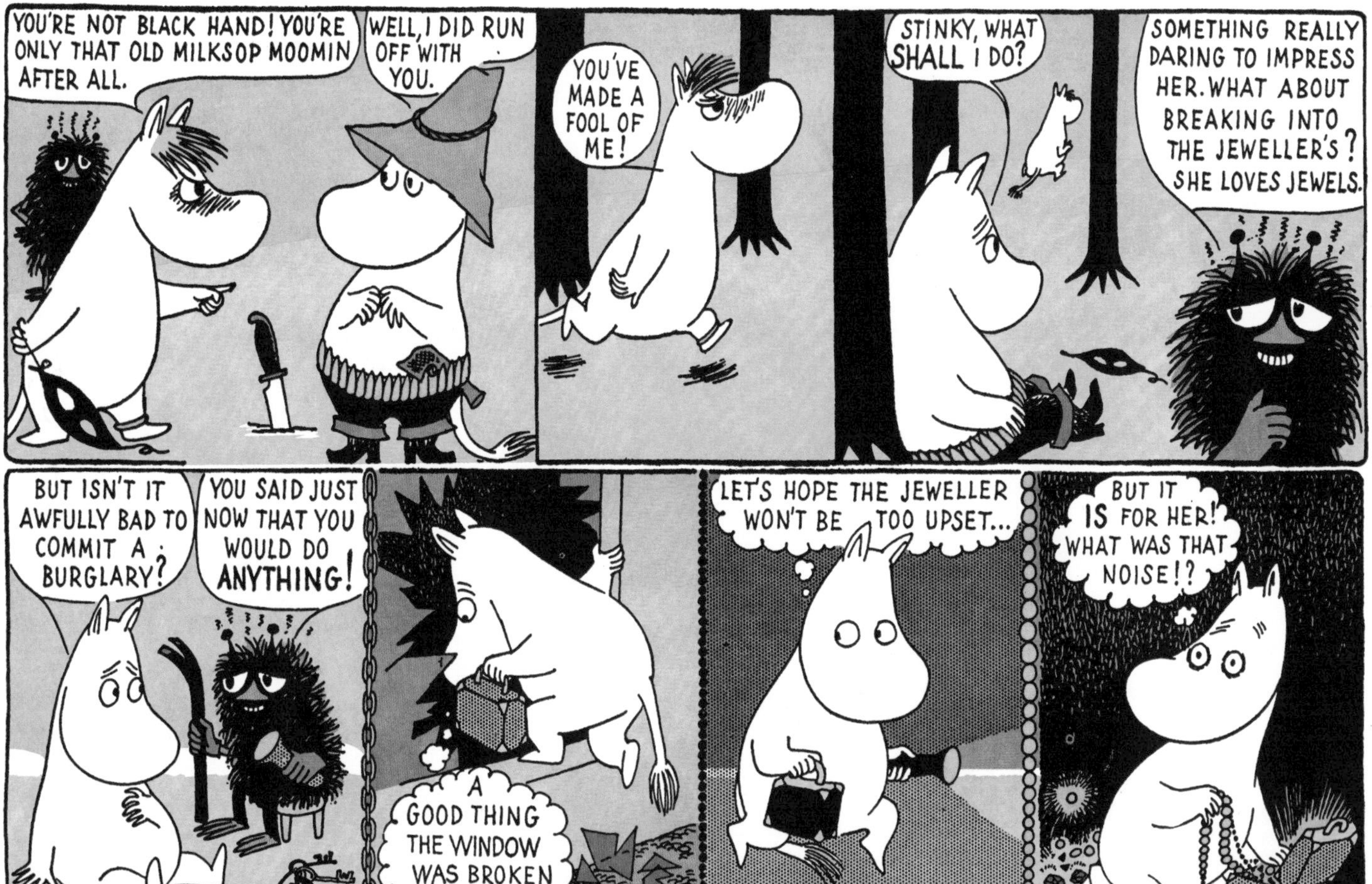

YOU'RE NOT BLACK HAND! YOU'RE ONLY THAT OLD MILKSOP MOOMIN AFTER ALL.
WELL, I DID RUN OFF WITH YOU.
YOU'VE MADE A FOOL OF ME!
STINKY, WHAT SHALL I DO?
SOMETHING REALLY DARING TO IMPRESS HER. WHAT ABOUT BREAKING INTO THE JEWELLER'S? SHE LOVES JEWELS.
BUT ISN'T IT AWFULLY BAD TO COMMIT A BURGLARY?
YOU SAID JUST NOW THAT YOU WOULD DO ANYTHING!
A GOOD THING THE WINDOW WAS BROKEN ALREADY...
LET'S HOPE THE JEWELLER WON'T BE TOO UPSET...
BUT IT IS FOR HER! WHAT WAS THAT NOISE!?

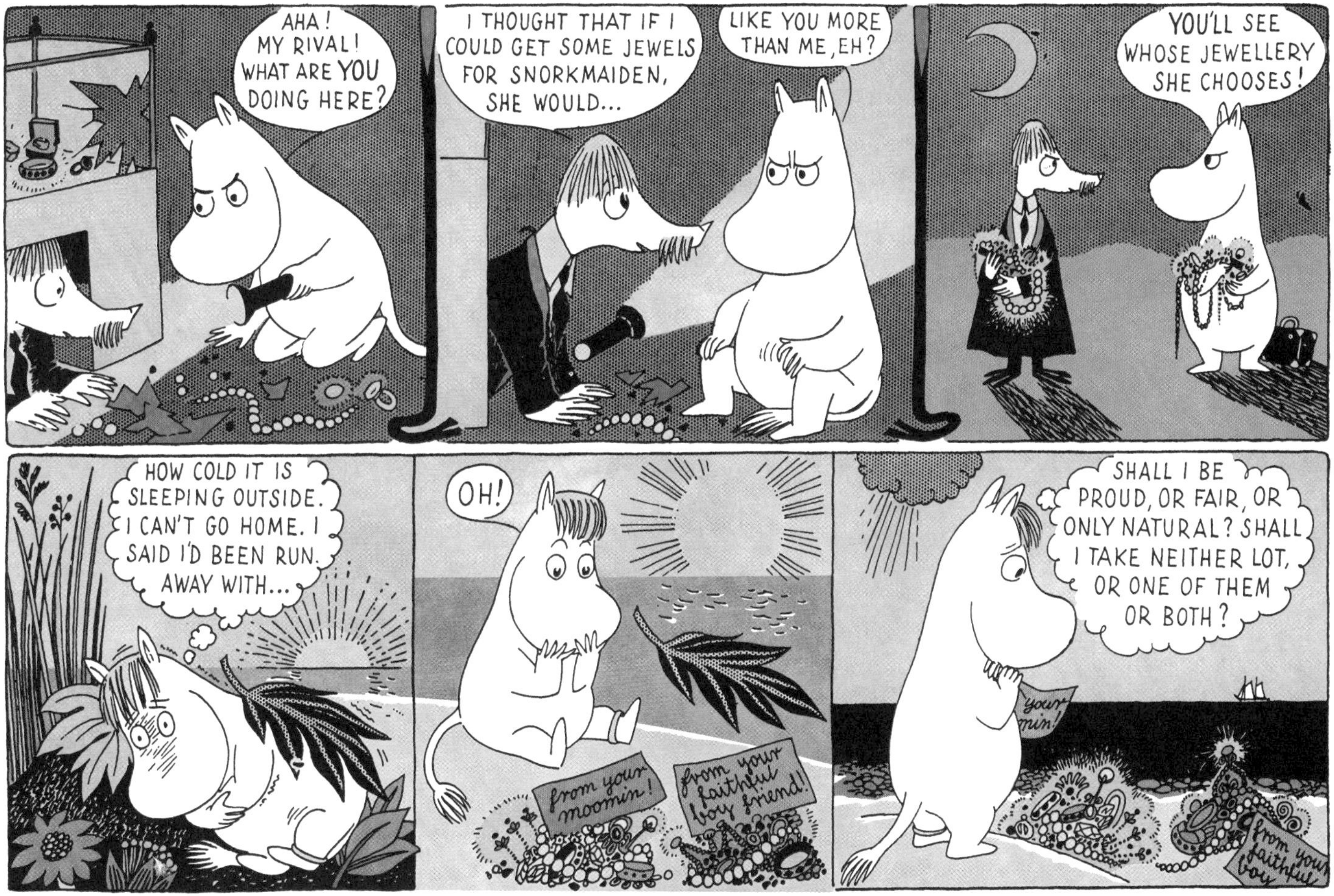
AHA! MY RIVAL! WHAT ARE YOU DOING HERE?
I THOUGHT THAT IF I COULD GET SOME JEWELS FOR SNORKMAIDEN, SHE WOULD...
LIKE YOU MORE THAN ME, EH?
YOU'LL SEE WHOSE JEWELLERY SHE CHOOSES!
HOW COLD IT IS SLEEPING OUTSIDE. I CAN'T GO HOME. I SAID I'D BEEN RUN AWAY WITH...
OH!
from your moomin!
from your faithful boy friend!
SHALL I BE PROUD, OR FAIR, OR ONLY NATURAL? SHALL I TAKE NEITHER LOT, OR ONE OF THEM OR BOTH?
from your faithful boy

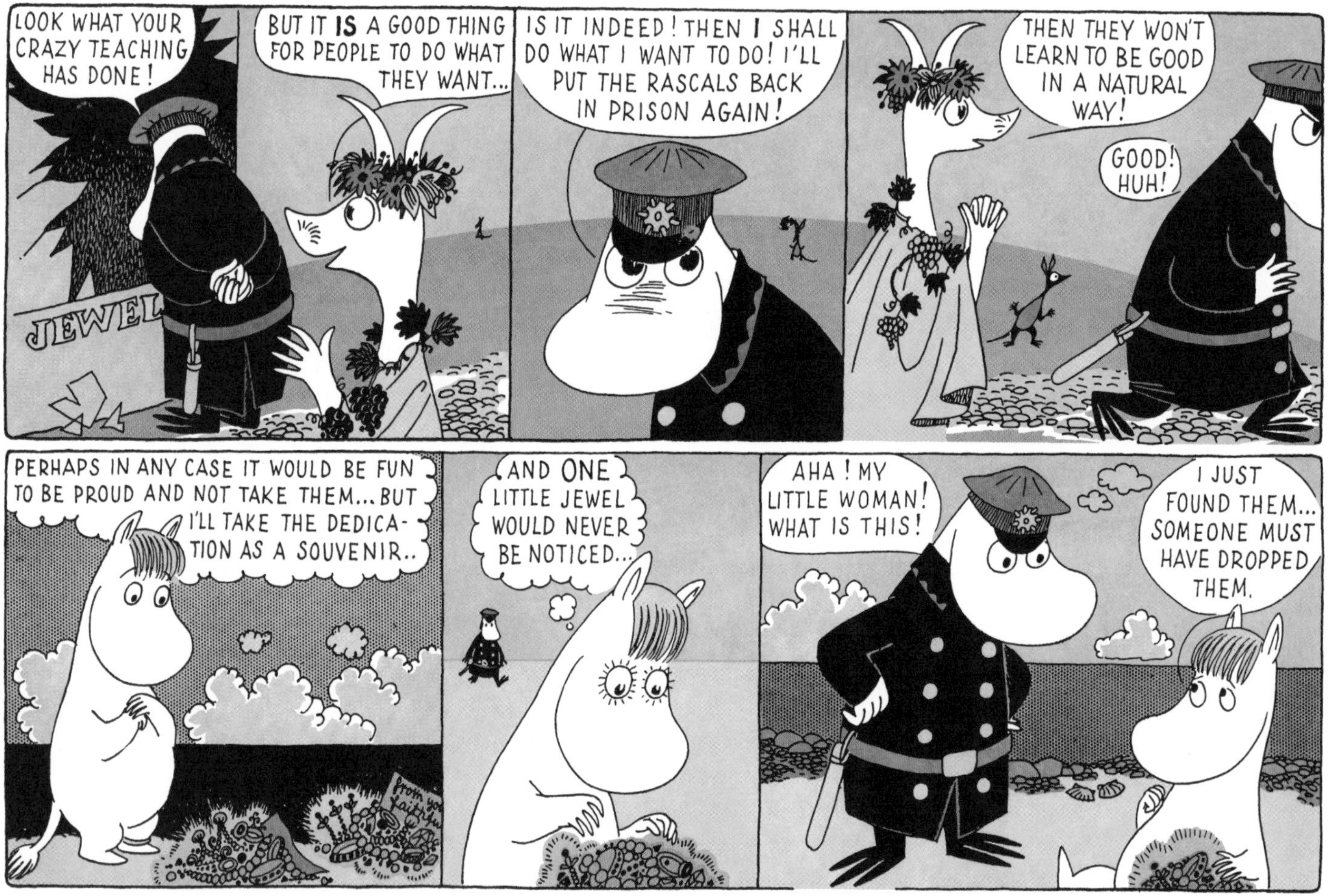
LOOK WHAT YOUR CRAZY TEACHING HAS DONE!
JEWEL
BUT IT **IS** A GOOD THING FOR PEOPLE TO DO WHAT THEY WANT...
IS IT INDEED! THEN **I** SHALL DO WHAT I WANT TO DO! I'LL PUT THE RASCALS BACK IN PRISON AGAIN!
THEN THEY WON'T LEARN TO BE GOOD IN A NATURAL WAY!
GOOD! HUH!
PERHAPS IN ANY CASE IT WOULD BE FUN TO BE PROUD AND NOT TAKE THEM... BUT I'LL TAKE THE DEDICATION AS A SOUVENIR..
AND ONE LITTLE JEWEL WOULD NEVER BE NOTICED...
AHA! MY LITTLE WOMAN! WHAT IS THIS!
I JUST FOUND THEM... SOMEONE MUST HAVE DROPPED THEM.

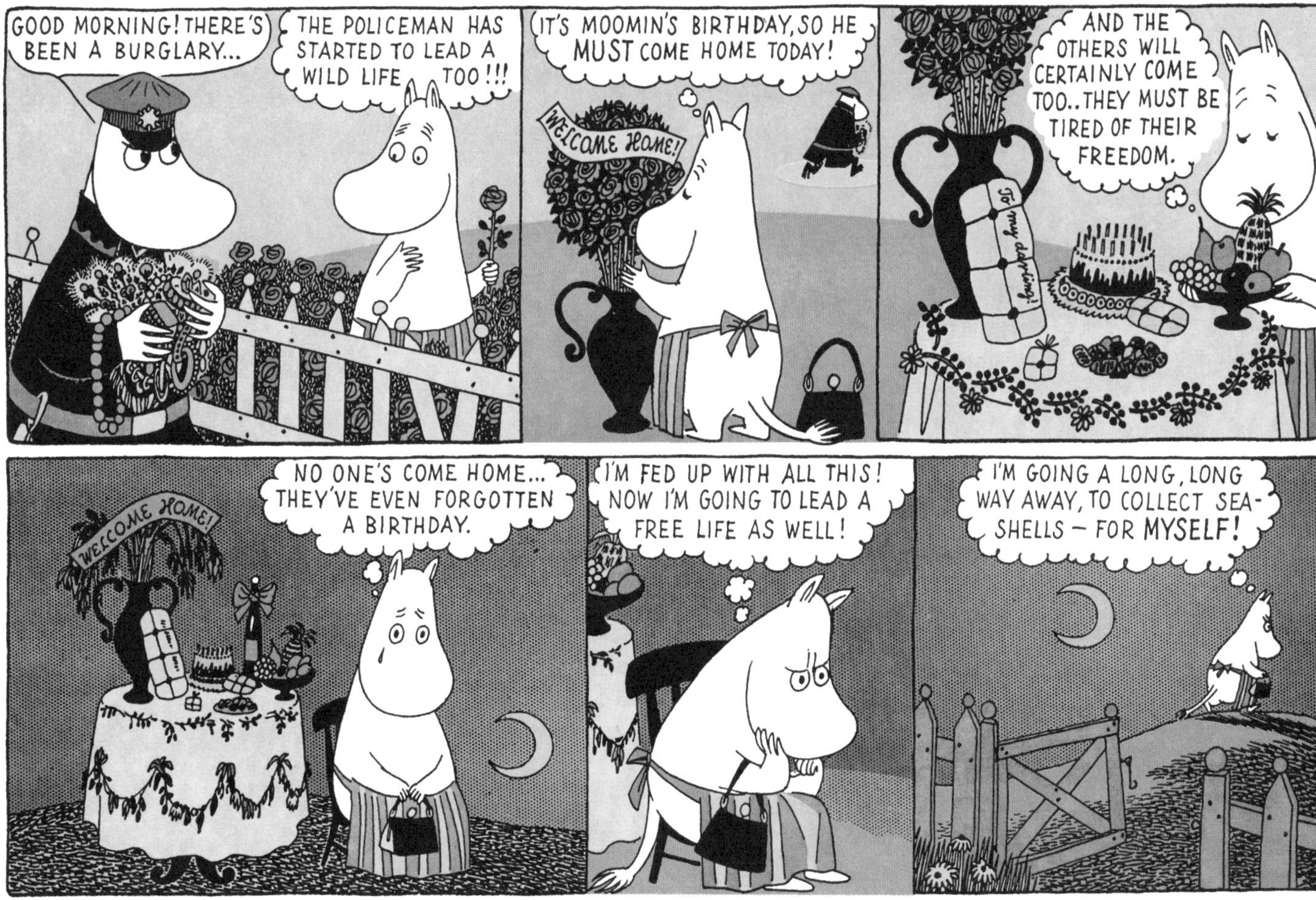
GOOD MORNING! THERE'S BEEN A BURGLARY...
THE POLICEMAN HAS STARTED TO LEAD A WILD LIFE TOO!!!
IT'S MOOMIN'S BIRTHDAY, SO HE MUST COME HOME TODAY!
WELCOME HOME!
AND THE OTHERS WILL CERTAINLY COME TOO.. THEY MUST BE TIRED OF THEIR FREEDOM.
To my darling!
NO ONE'S COME HOME... THEY'VE EVEN FORGOTTEN A BIRTHDAY.
WELCOME HOME!
I'M FED UP WITH ALL THIS! NOW I'M GOING TO LEAD A FREE LIFE AS WELL!
I'M GOING A LONG, LONG WAY AWAY, TO COLLECT SEA-SHELLS – FOR MYSELF!

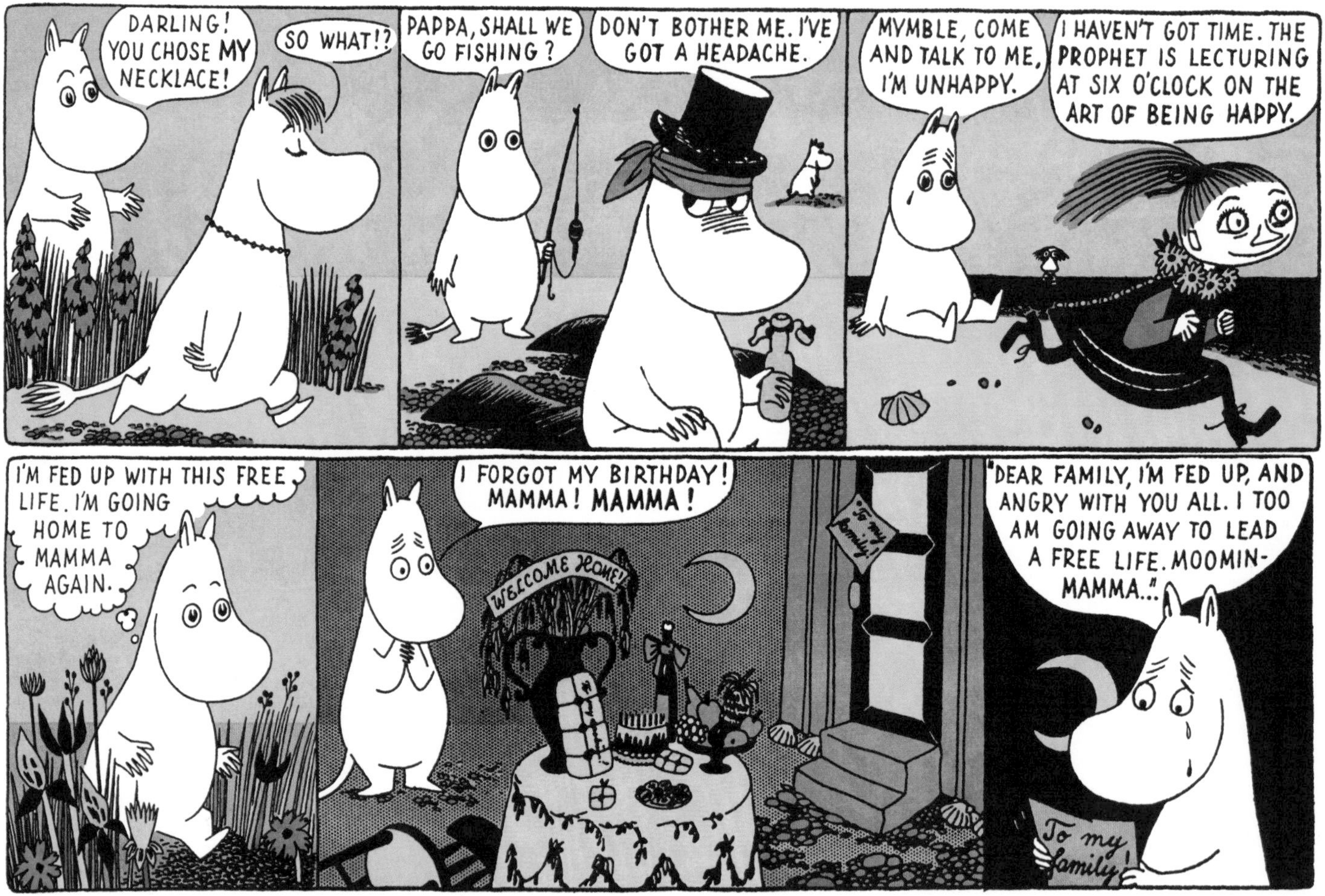
DARLING! YOU CHOSE MY NECKLACE!
SO WHAT!?
PAPPA, SHALL WE GO FISHING?
DON'T BOTHER ME. I'VE GOT A HEADACHE.
MYMBLE, COME AND TALK TO ME, I'M UNHAPPY.
I HAVEN'T GOT TIME. THE PROPHET IS LECTURING AT SIX O'CLOCK ON THE ART OF BEING HAPPY.
I'M FED UP WITH THIS FREE LIFE. I'M GOING HOME TO MAMMA AGAIN.
I FORGOT MY BIRTHDAY! MAMMA! MAMMA!
WELCOME HOME!
To my family!
"DEAR FAMILY, I'M FED UP, AND ANGRY WITH YOU ALL. I TOO AM GOING AWAY TO LEAD A FREE LIFE. MOOMIN-MAMMA..."
To my family!

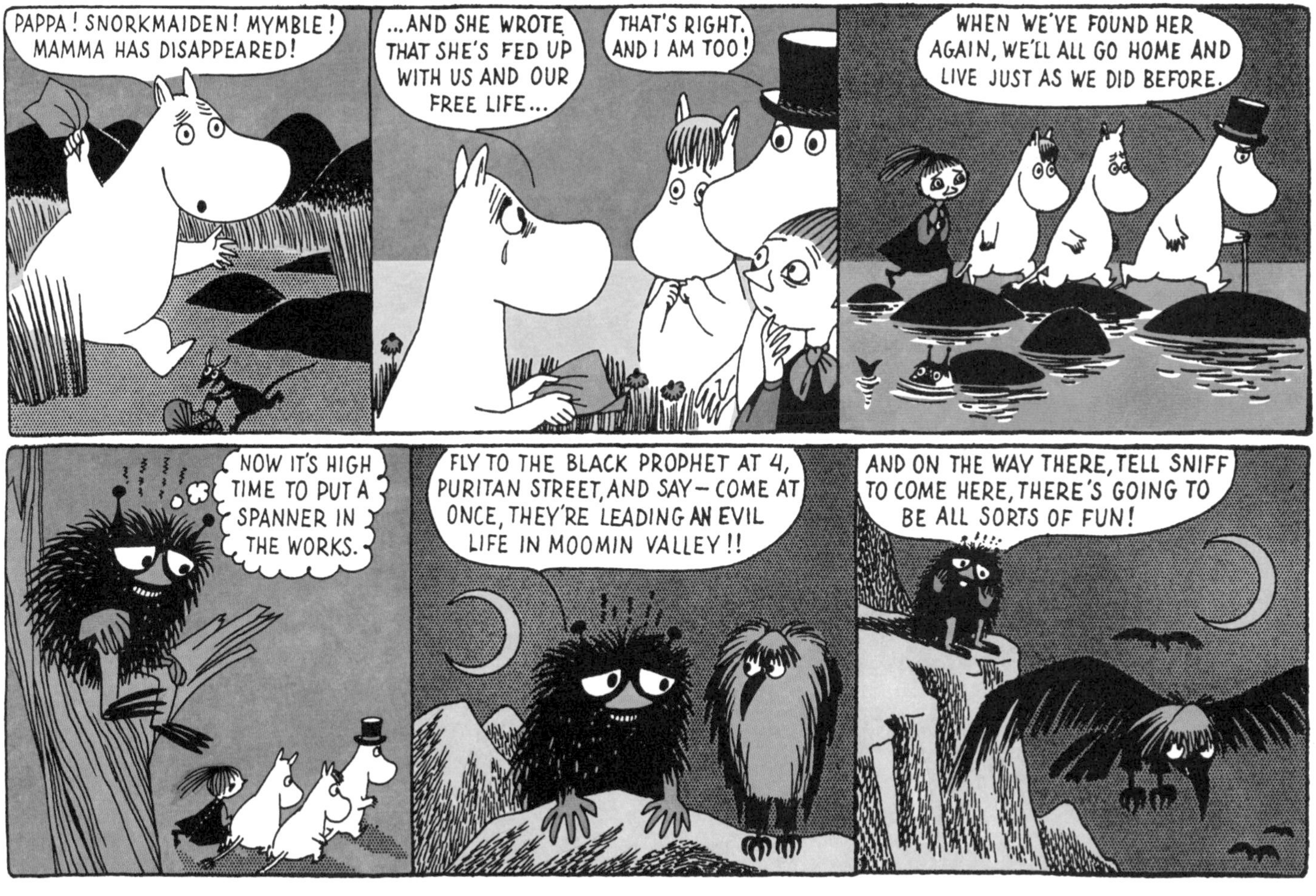
PAPPA! SNORKMAIDEN! MYMBLE! MAMMA HAS DISAPPEARED!
...AND SHE WROTE THAT SHE'S FED UP WITH US AND OUR FREE LIFE...
THAT'S RIGHT. AND I AM TOO!
WHEN WE'VE FOUND HER AGAIN, WE'LL ALL GO HOME AND LIVE JUST AS WE DID BEFORE.
NOW IT'S HIGH TIME TO PUT A SPANNER IN THE WORKS.
FLY TO THE BLACK PROPHET AT 4, PURITAN STREET, AND SAY – COME AT ONCE, THEY'RE LEADING AN EVIL LIFE IN MOOMIN VALLEY!!
AND ON THE WAY THERE, TELL SNIFF TO COME HERE, THERE'S GOING TO BE ALL SORTS OF FUN!

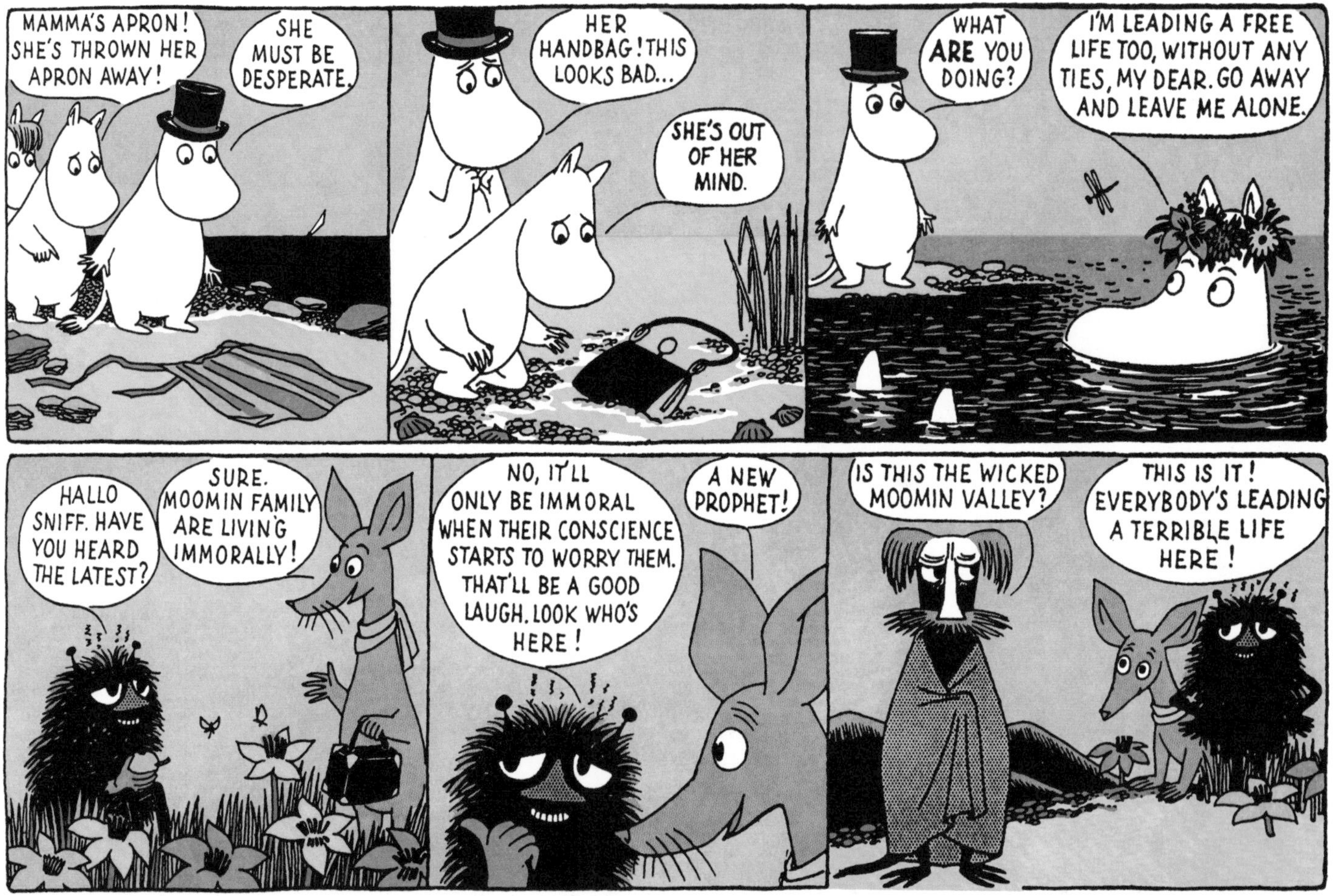
MAMMA'S APRON! SHE'S THROWN HER APRON AWAY!
SHE MUST BE DESPERATE.
HER HANDBAG! THIS LOOKS BAD...
SHE'S OUT OF HER MIND.
WHAT **ARE** YOU DOING?
I'M LEADING A FREE LIFE TOO, WITHOUT ANY TIES, MY DEAR. GO AWAY AND LEAVE ME ALONE.
HALLO SNIFF. HAVE YOU HEARD THE LATEST?
SURE. MOOMIN FAMILY ARE LIVING IMMORALLY!
NO, IT'LL ONLY BE IMMORAL WHEN THEIR CONSCIENCE STARTS TO WORRY THEM. THAT'LL BE A GOOD LAUGH. LOOK WHO'S HERE!
A NEW PROPHET!
IS THIS THE WICKED MOOMIN VALLEY?
THIS IS IT! EVERYBODY'S LEADING A TERRIBLE LIFE HERE!

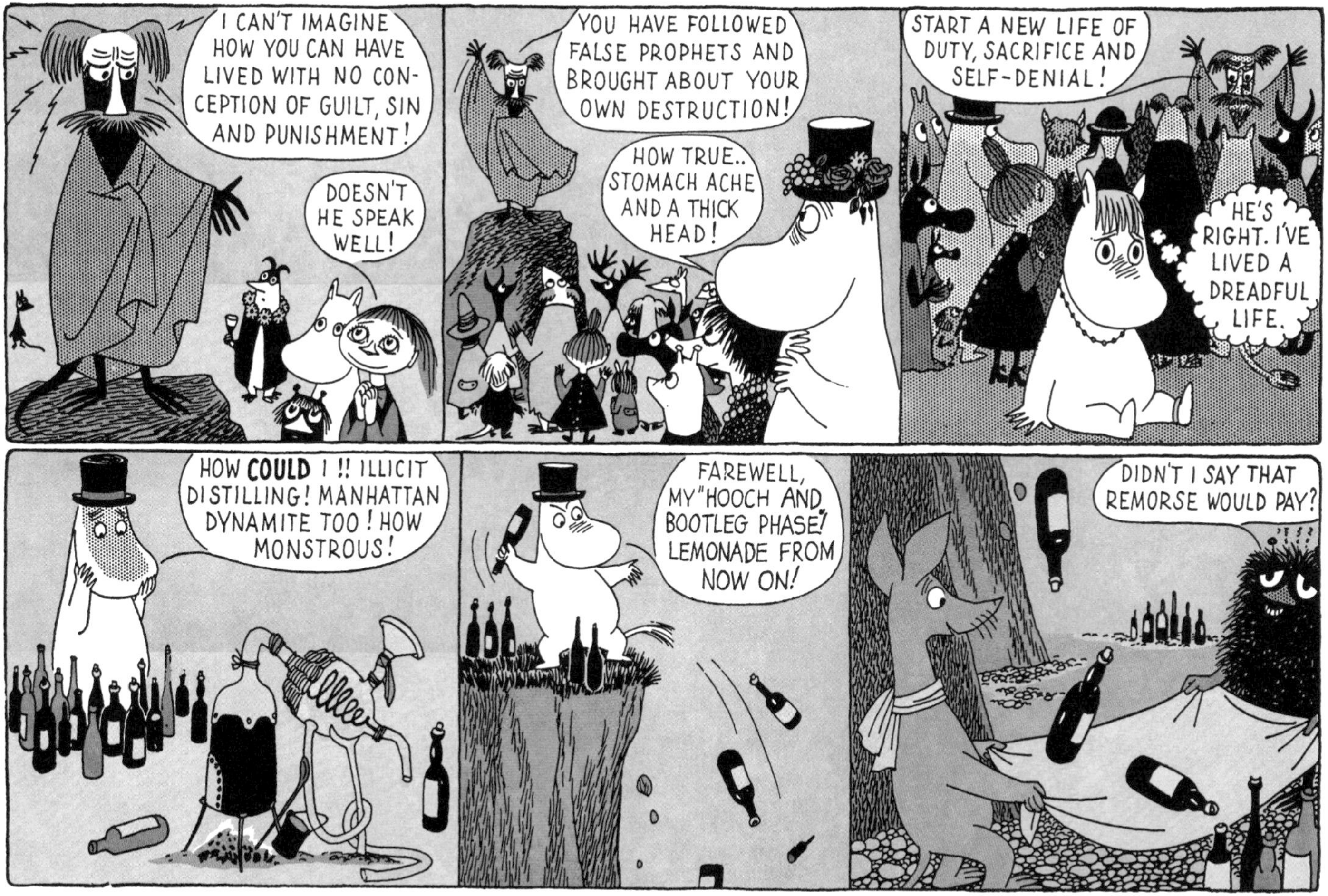
I CAN'T IMAGINE HOW YOU CAN HAVE LIVED WITH NO CONCEPTION OF GUILT, SIN AND PUNISHMENT!
DOESN'T HE SPEAK WELL!
YOU HAVE FOLLOWED FALSE PROPHETS AND BROUGHT ABOUT YOUR OWN DESTRUCTION!
HOW TRUE.. STOMACH ACHE AND A THICK HEAD!
START A NEW LIFE OF DUTY, SACRIFICE AND SELF-DENIAL!
HE'S RIGHT. I'VE LIVED A DREADFUL LIFE.
HOW **COULD** I !! ILLICIT DISTILLING! MANHATTAN DYNAMITE TOO! HOW MONSTROUS!
FAREWELL, MY "HOOCH AND BOOTLEG PHASE"! LEMONADE FROM NOW ON!
DIDN'T I SAY THAT REMORSE WOULD PAY?

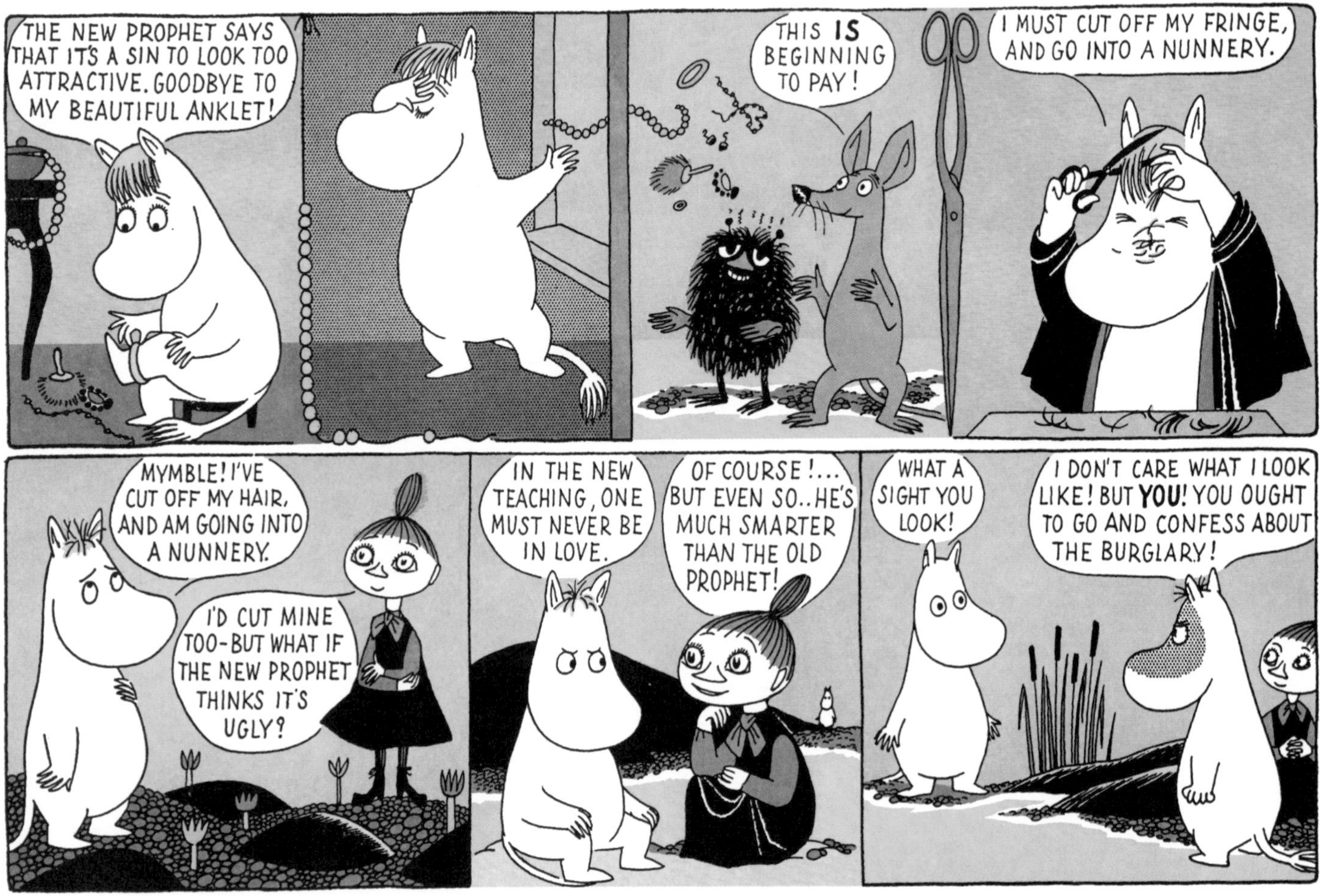
THE NEW PROPHET SAYS THAT IT'S A SIN TO LOOK TOO ATTRACTIVE. GOODBYE TO MY BEAUTIFUL ANKLET!
THIS **IS** BEGINNING TO PAY!
I MUST CUT OFF MY FRINGE, AND GO INTO A NUNNERY.
MYMBLE! I'VE CUT OFF MY HAIR, AND AM GOING INTO A NUNNERY.
I'D CUT MINE TOO-BUT WHAT IF THE NEW PROPHET THINKS IT'S UGLY?
IN THE NEW TEACHING, ONE MUST NEVER BE IN LOVE.
OF COURSE!... BUT EVEN SO..HE'S MUCH SMARTER THAN THE OLD PROPHET!
WHAT A SIGHT YOU LOOK!
I DON'T CARE WHAT I LOOK LIKE! BUT **YOU**! YOU OUGHT TO GO AND CONFESS ABOUT THE BURGLARY!

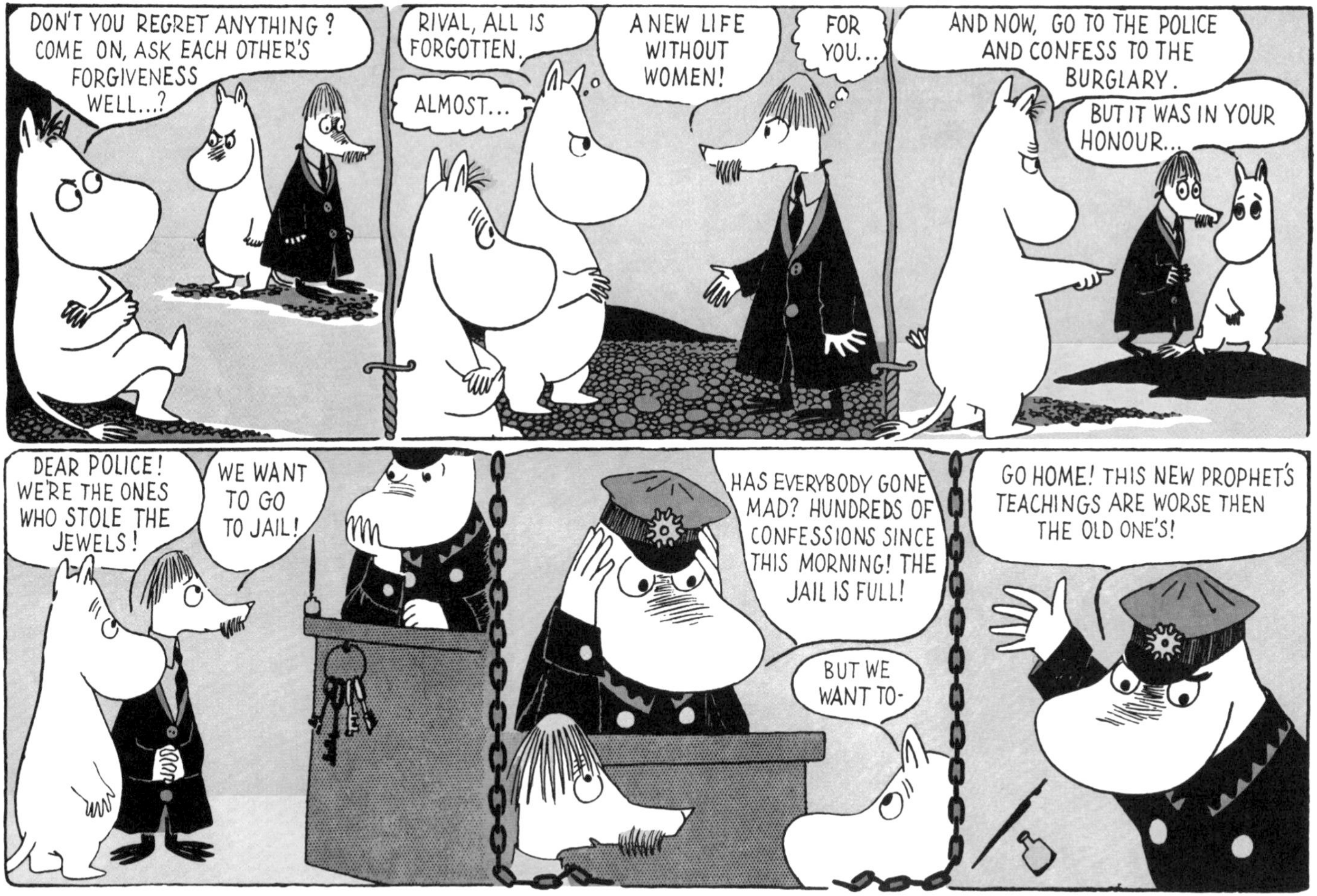
DON'T YOU REGRET ANYTHING? COME ON, ASK EACH OTHER'S FORGIVENESS WELL...?
RIVAL, ALL IS FORGOTTEN.
ALMOST...
A NEW LIFE WITHOUT WOMEN!
FOR YOU...
AND NOW, GO TO THE POLICE AND CONFESS TO THE BURGLARY.
BUT IT WAS IN YOUR HONOUR...
DEAR POLICE! WE'RE THE ONES WHO STOLE THE JEWELS!
WE WANT TO GO TO JAIL!
HAS EVERYBODY GONE MAD? HUNDREDS OF CONFESSIONS SINCE THIS MORNING! THE JAIL IS FULL!
BUT WE WANT TO-
GO HOME! THIS NEW PROPHET'S TEACHINGS ARE WORSE THEN THE OLD ONE'S!

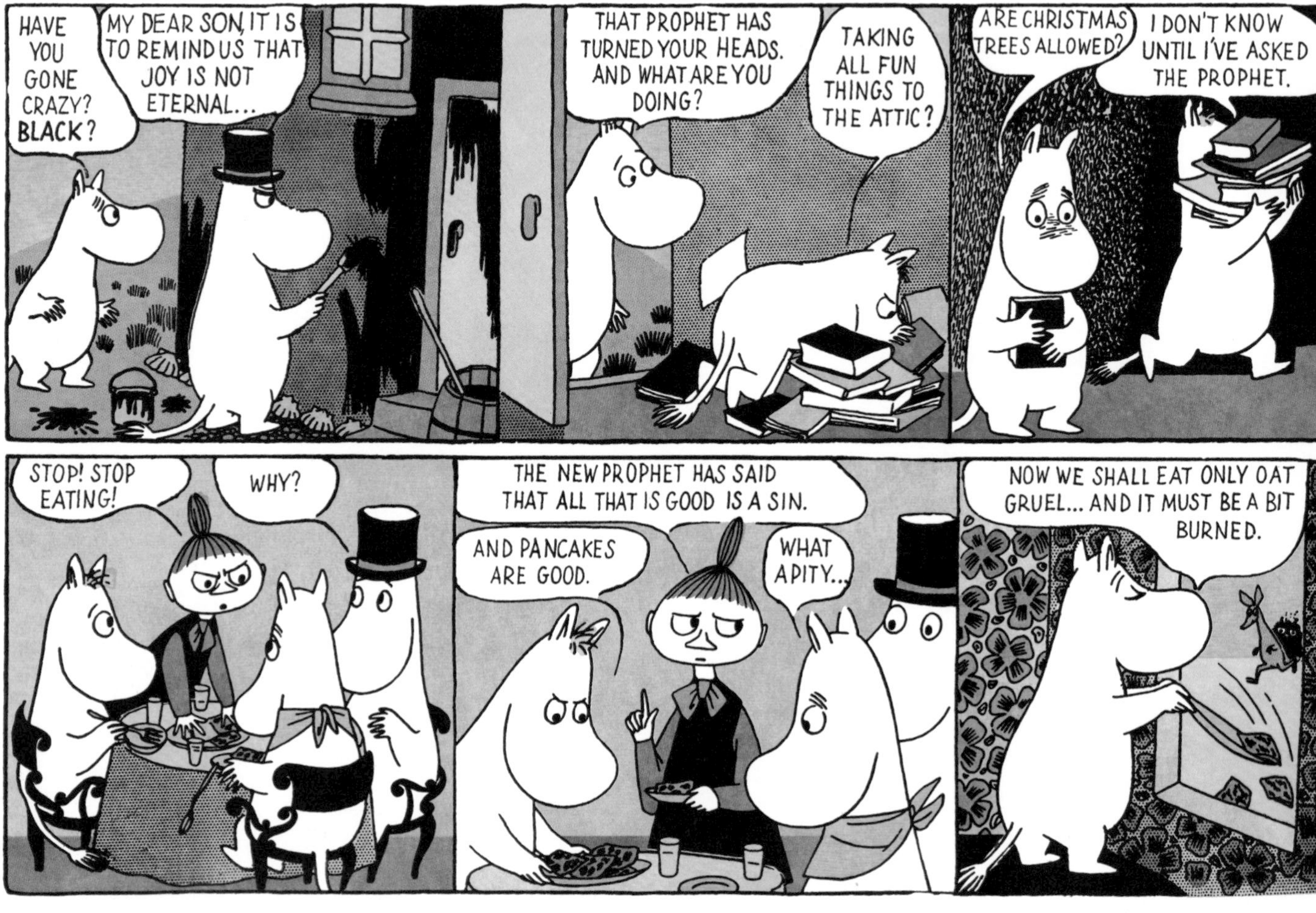
HAVE YOU GONE CRAZY? BLACK?
MY DEAR SON, IT IS TO REMIND US THAT JOY IS NOT ETERNAL...
THAT PROPHET HAS TURNED YOUR HEADS. AND WHAT ARE YOU DOING?
TAKING ALL FUN THINGS TO THE ATTIC?
ARE CHRISTMAS TREES ALLOWED?
I DON'T KNOW UNTIL I'VE ASKED THE PROPHET.
STOP! STOP EATING!
WHY?
THE NEW PROPHET HAS SAID THAT ALL THAT IS GOOD IS A SIN.
AND PANCAKES ARE GOOD.
WHAT A PITY...
NOW WE SHALL EAT ONLY OAT GRUEL... AND IT MUST BE A BIT BURNED.

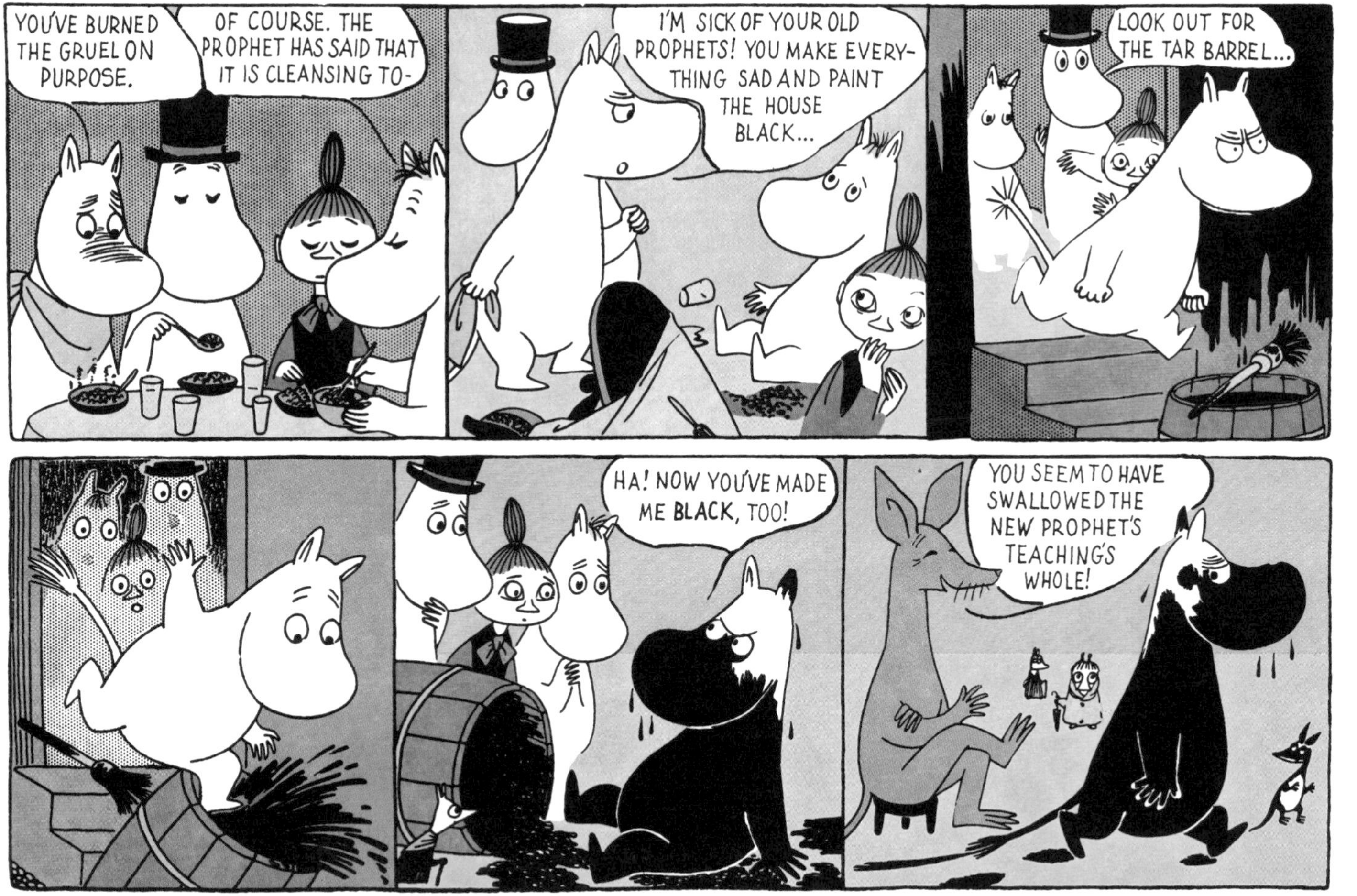
YOU'VE BURNED THE GRUEL ON PURPOSE.
OF COURSE. THE PROPHET HAS SAID THAT IT IS CLEANSING TO-
I'M SICK OF YOUR OLD PROPHETS! YOU MAKE EVERY-THING SAD AND PAINT THE HOUSE BLACK...
LOOK OUT FOR THE TAR BARREL...
HA! NOW YOU'VE MADE ME BLACK, TOO!
YOU SEEM TO HAVE SWALLOWED THE NEW PROPHET'S TEACHING'S WHOLE!

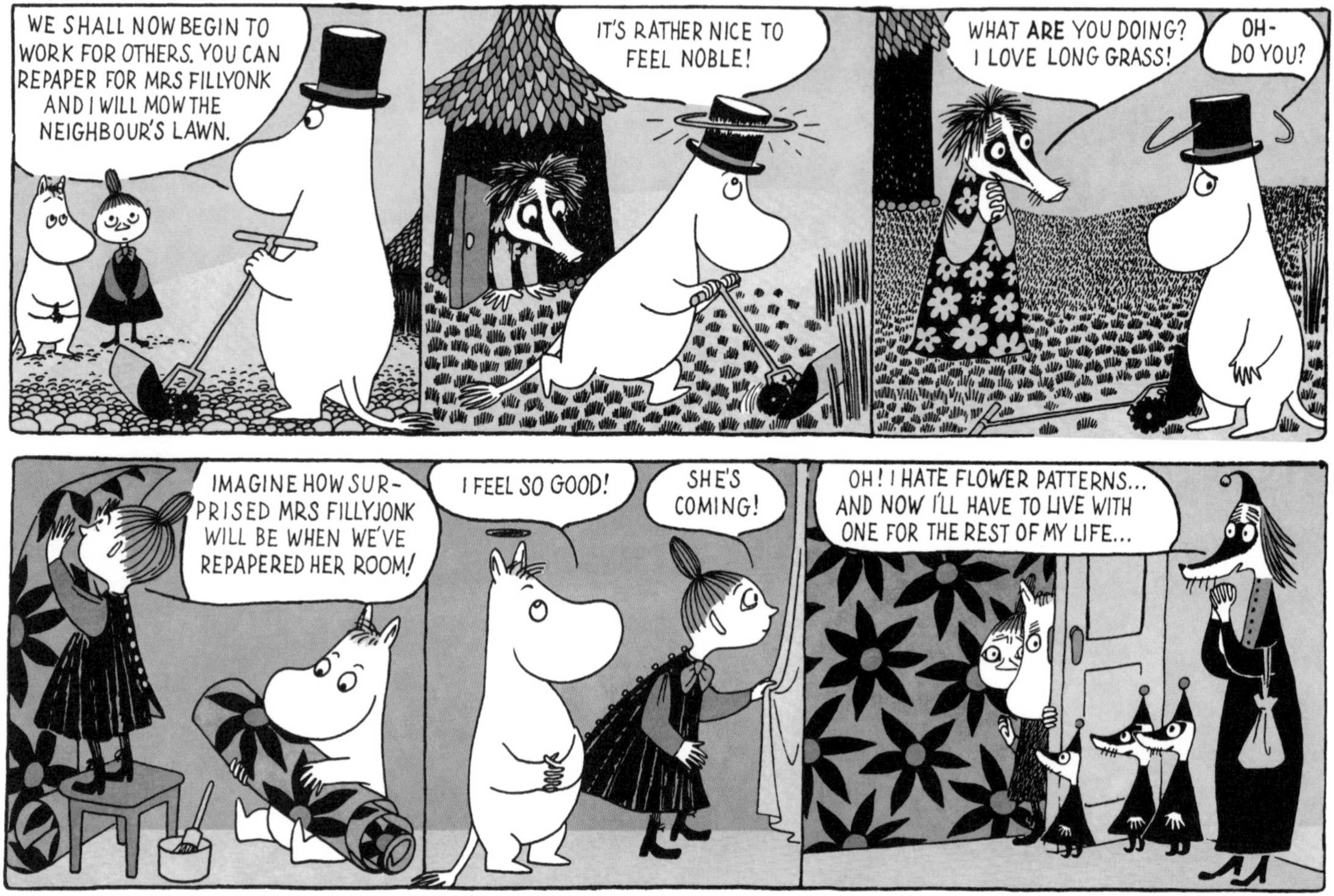
WE SHALL NOW BEGIN TO WORK FOR OTHERS. YOU CAN REPAPER FOR MRS FILLYONK AND I WILL MOW THE NEIGHBOUR'S LAWN.
IT'S RATHER NICE TO FEEL NOBLE!
WHAT **ARE** YOU DOING? I LOVE LONG GRASS!
OH- DO YOU?
IMAGINE HOW SURPRISED MRS FILLYJONK WILL BE WHEN WE'VE REPAPERED HER ROOM!
I FEEL SO GOOD!
SHE'S COMING!
OH! I HATE FLOWER PATTERNS... AND NOW I'LL HAVE TO LIVE WITH ONE FOR THE REST OF MY LIFE...

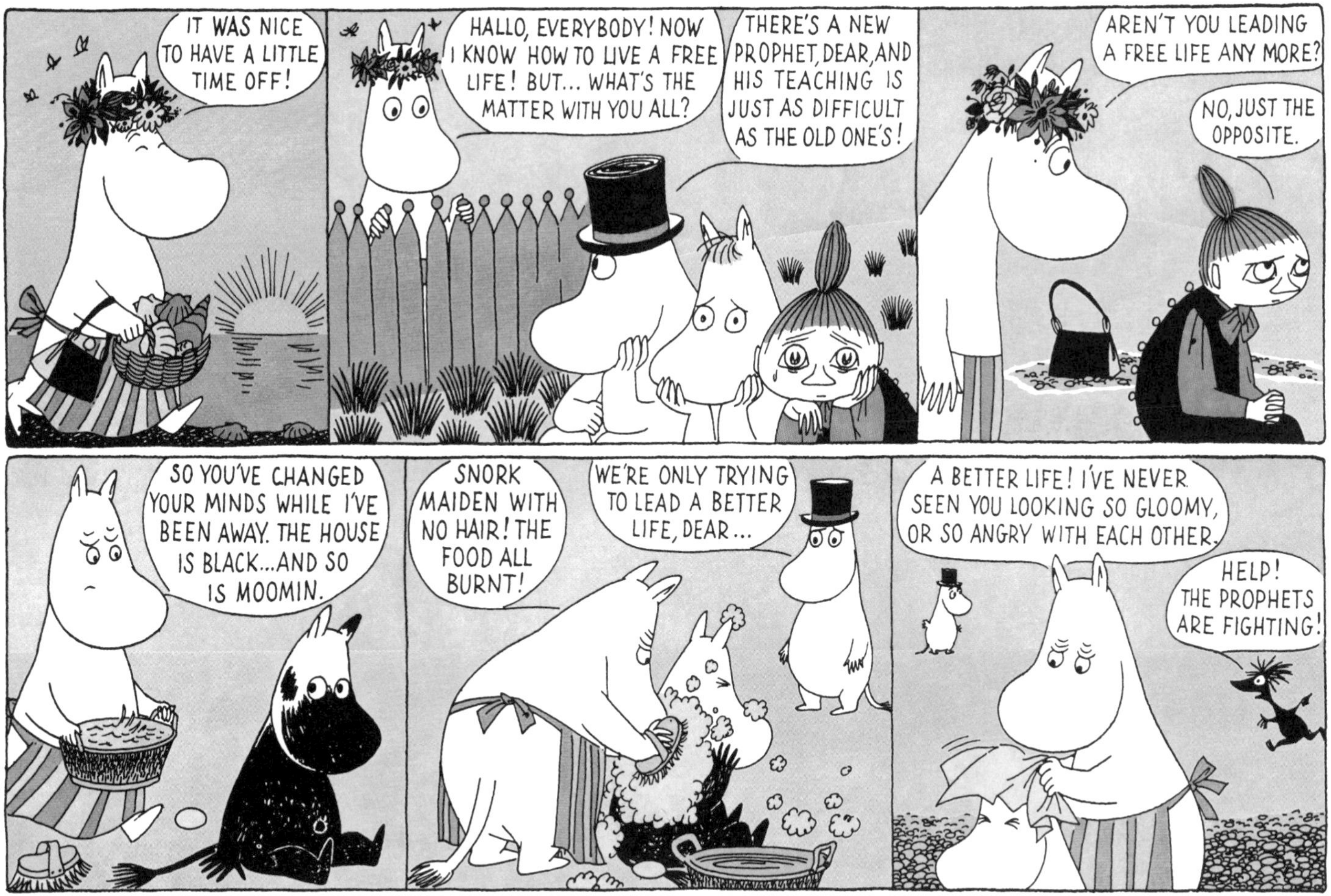
IT WAS NICE TO HAVE A LITTLE TIME OFF!
HALLO, EVERYBODY! NOW I KNOW HOW TO LIVE A FREE LIFE! BUT... WHAT'S THE MATTER WITH YOU ALL?
THERE'S A NEW PROPHET, DEAR, AND HIS TEACHING IS JUST AS DIFFICULT AS THE OLD ONE'S!
AREN'T YOU LEADING A FREE LIFE ANY MORE?
NO, JUST THE OPPOSITE.
SO YOU'VE CHANGED YOUR MINDS WHILE I'VE BEEN AWAY. THE HOUSE IS BLACK...AND SO IS MOOMIN.
SNORK MAIDEN WITH NO HAIR! THE FOOD ALL BURNT!
WE'RE ONLY TRYING TO LEAD A BETTER LIFE, DEAR...
A BETTER LIFE! I'VE NEVER SEEN YOU LOOKING SO GLOOMY, OR SO ANGRY WITH EACH OTHER.
HELP! THE PROPHETS ARE FIGHTING!

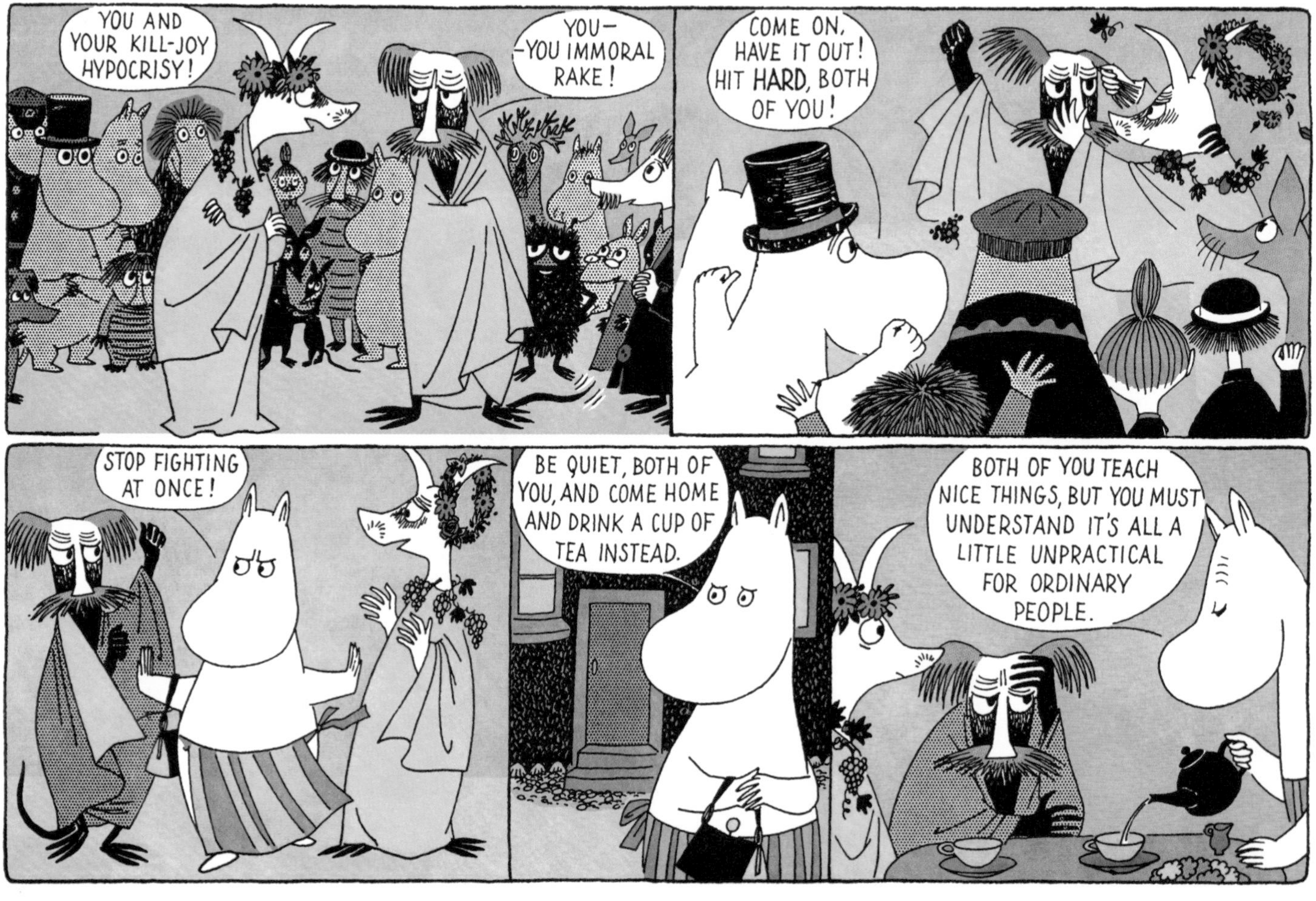
YOU AND YOUR KILL-JOY HYPOCRISY!
YOU— —YOU IMMORAL RAKE!
COME ON, HAVE IT OUT! HIT **HARD**, BOTH OF YOU!
STOP FIGHTING AT ONCE!
BE QUIET, BOTH OF YOU, AND COME HOME AND DRINK A CUP OF TEA INSTEAD.
BOTH OF YOU TEACH NICE THINGS, BUT YOU MUST UNDERSTAND IT'S ALL A LITTLE UNPRACTICAL FOR ORDINARY PEOPLE.

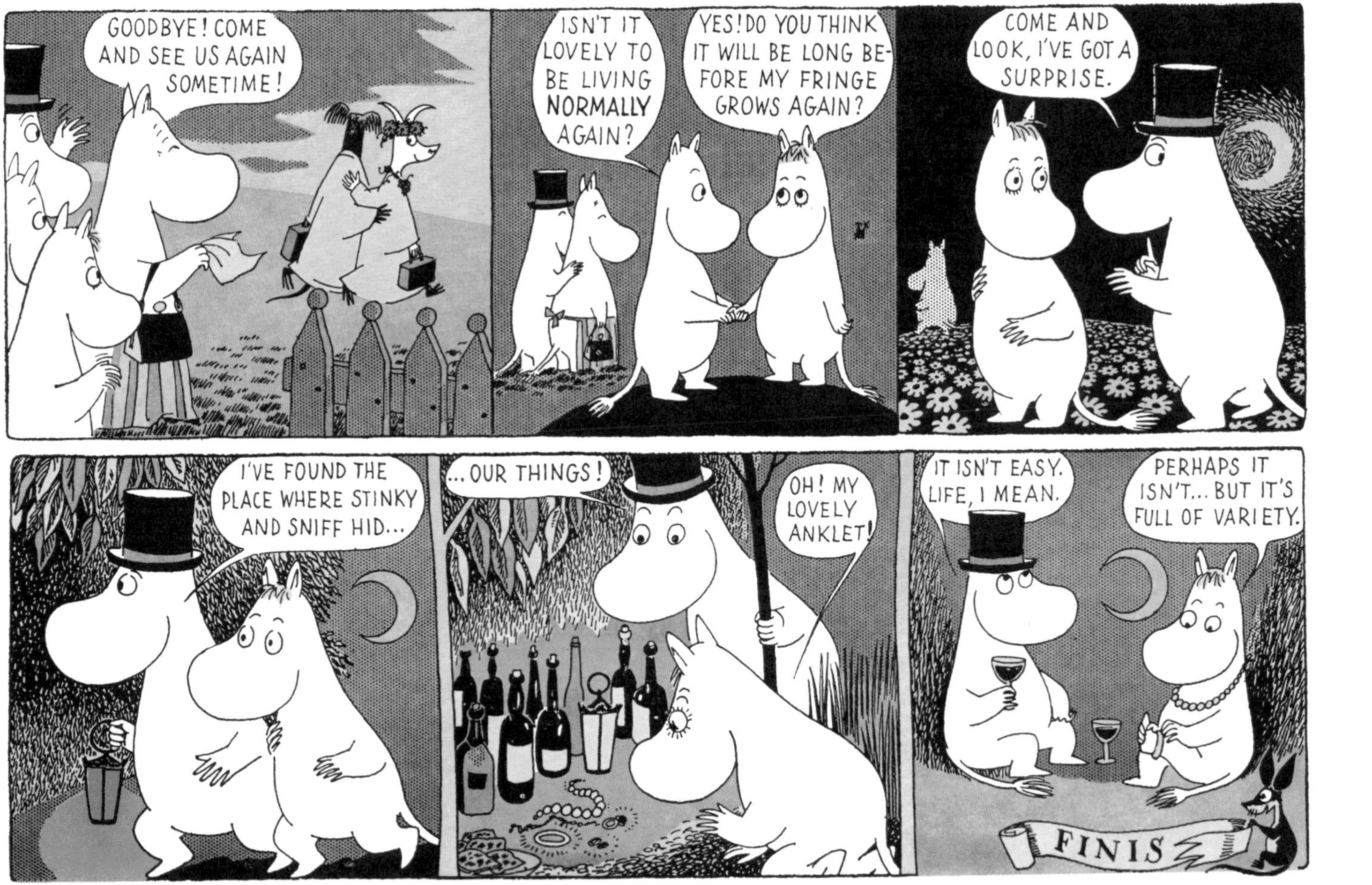
GOODBYE! COME AND SEE US AGAIN SOMETIME!
ISN'T IT LOVELY TO BE LIVING NORMALLY AGAIN?
YES! DO YOU THINK IT WILL BE LONG BEFORE MY FRINGE GROWS AGAIN?
COME AND LOOK, I'VE GOT A SURPRISE.
I'VE FOUND THE PLACE WHERE STINKY AND SNIFF HID...
...OUR THINGS!
OH! MY LOVELY ANKLET!
IT ISN'T EASY. LIFE, I MEAN.
PERHAPS IT ISN'T... BUT IT'S FULL OF VARIETY.
FINIS

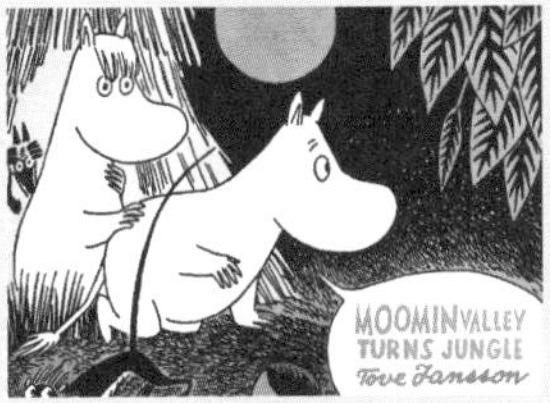
MOOMINVALLEY TURNS JUNGLE
Tove Jansson
Moominvalley Turns Jungle

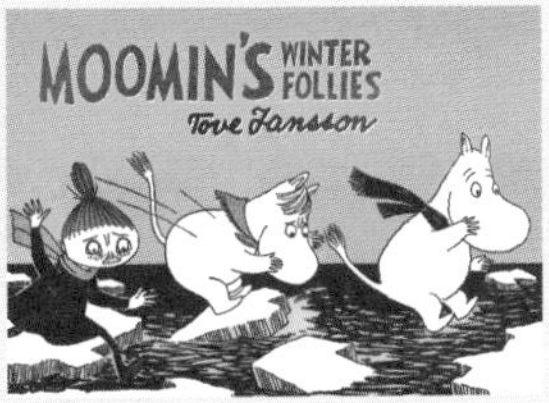
MOOMIN'S WINTER FOLLIES
Tove Jansson
Moomin's Winter Follies

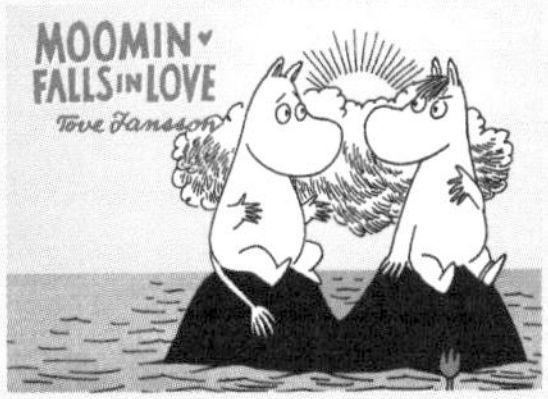
MOOMIN FALLS IN LOVE
Tove Jansson
Moomin Falls in Love

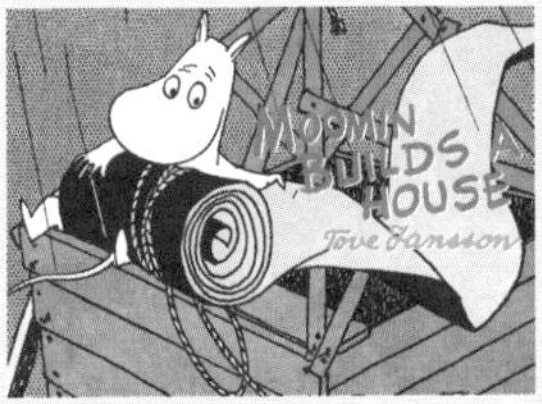
MOOMIN BUILDS A HOUSE
Tove Jansson
Moomin Builds a House

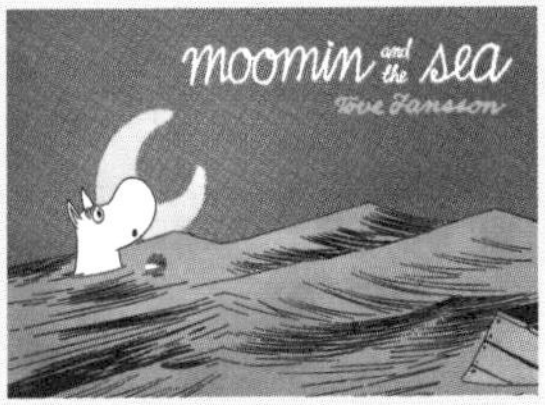
moomin and the sea
Tove Jansson
Moomin and the Sea

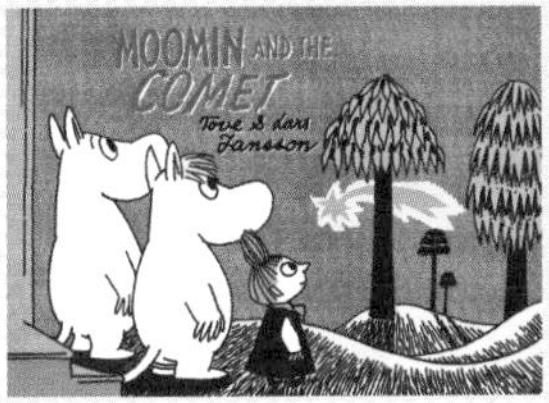
MOOMIN AND THE COMET
Tove & Lars Jansson
Moomin and the Comet

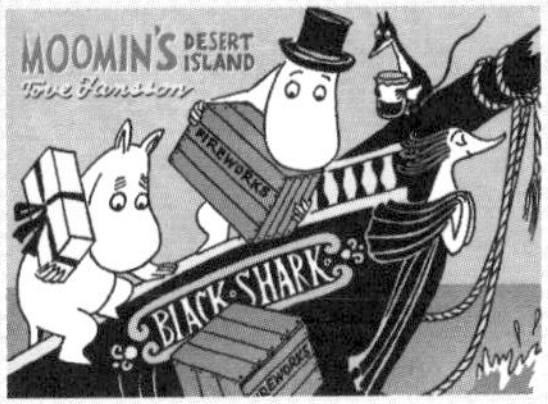
MOOMIN'S DESERT ISLAND
Tove Jansson
FIREWORKS
BLACK SHARK
Moomin's Desert Island

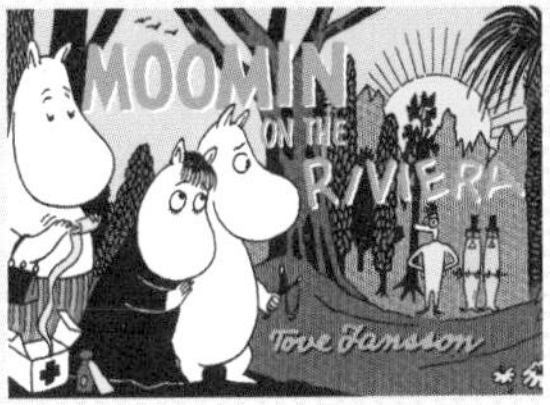
MOOMIN ON THE RIVIERA
Tove Jansson
Moomin on the Riviera

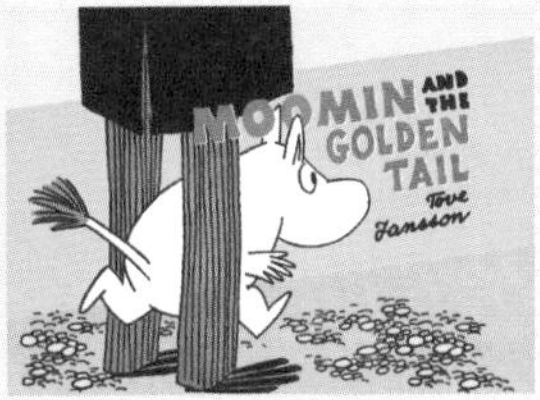
MOOMIN AND THE GOLDEN TAIL
Tove Jansson
Moomin and the Golden Tail

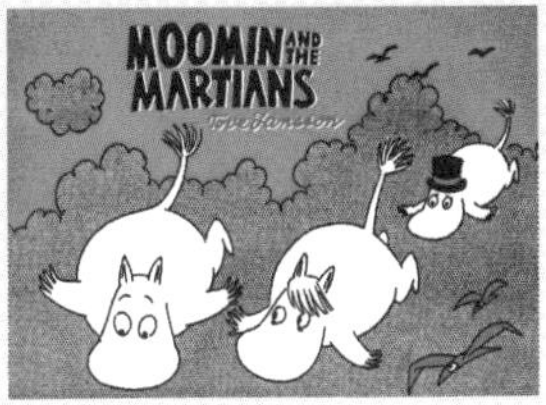
MOOMIN AND THE MARTIANS
Tove Jansson
Moomin and the Martians

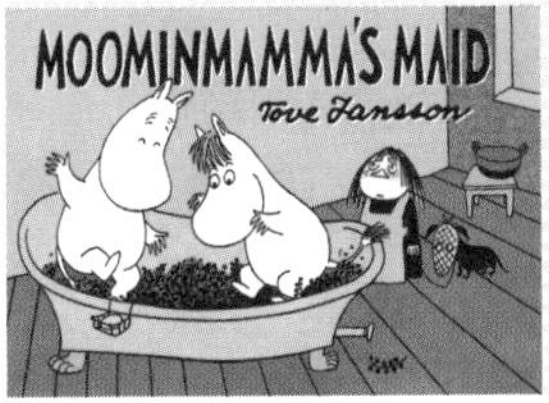
MOOMINMAMMA'S MAID
Tove Jansson
Moominmamma's Maid

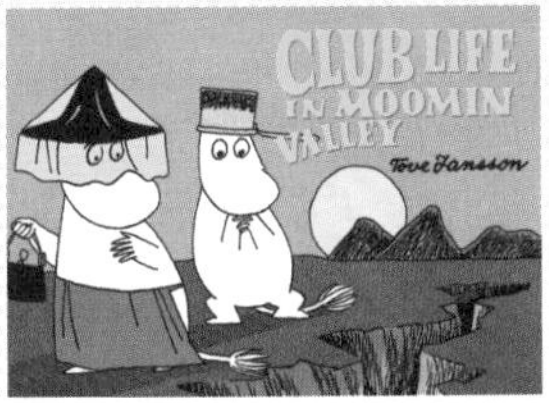
CLUB LIFE IN MOOMIN VALLEY
Tove Jansson
Club Life in Moominvalley

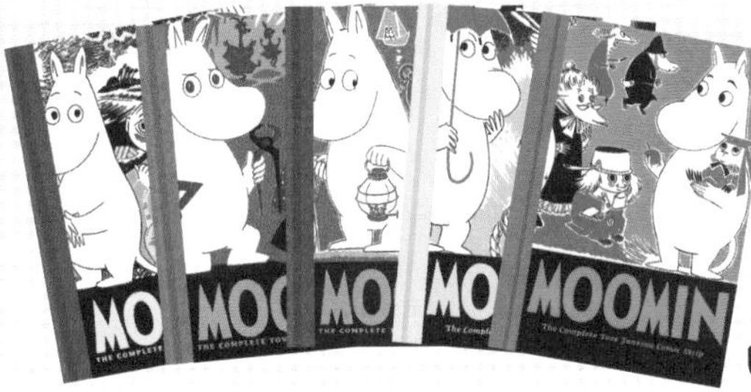
MOOMIN

Also available
THE TOVE AND LARS JANSSON CLASSIC HARDCOVERS

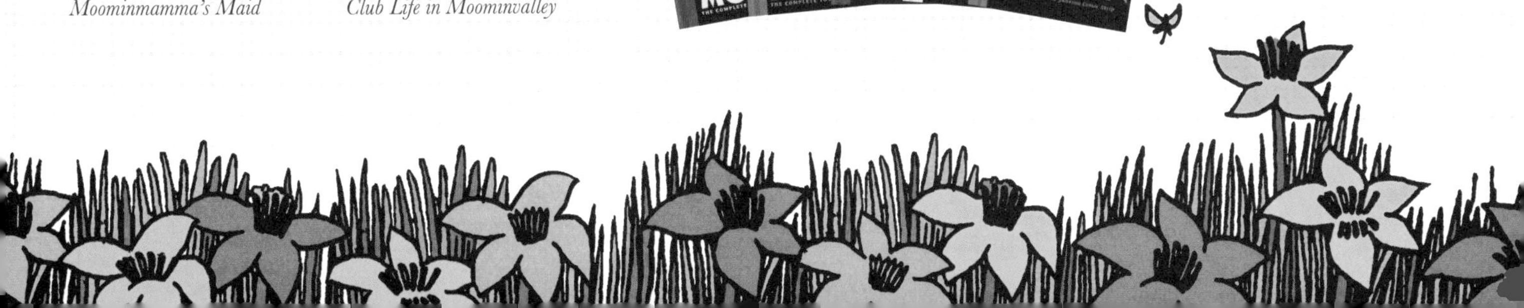

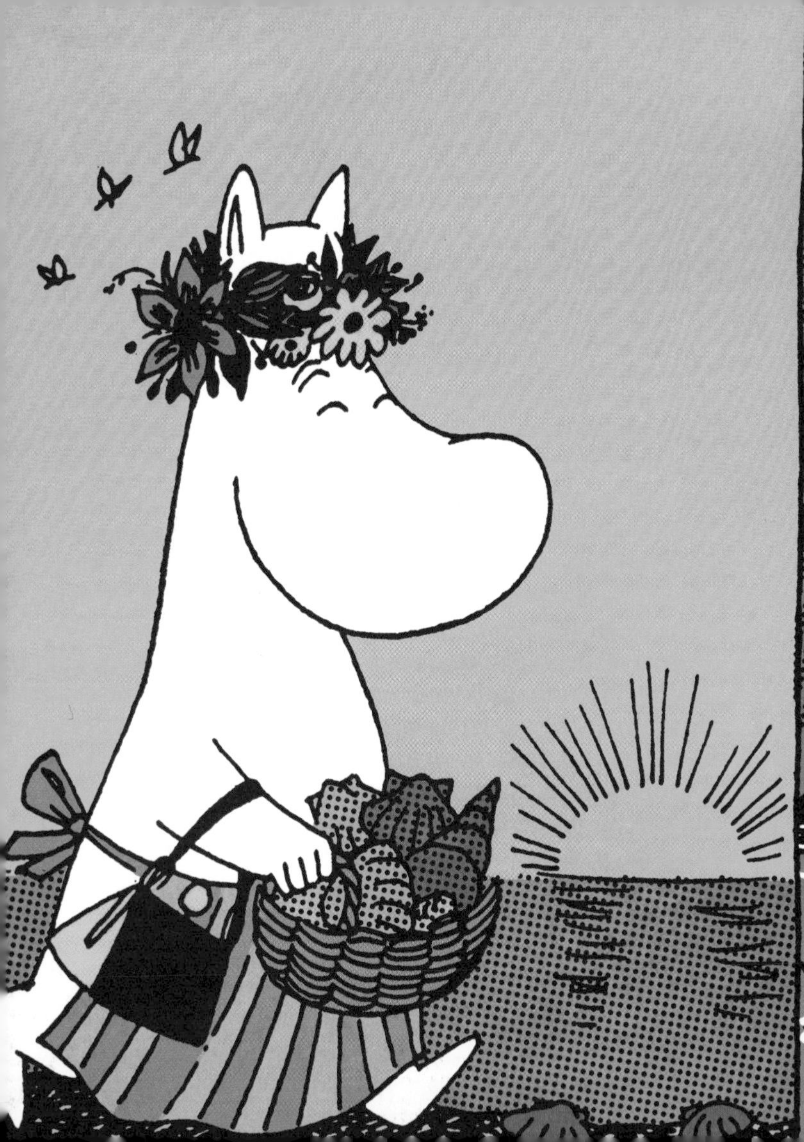
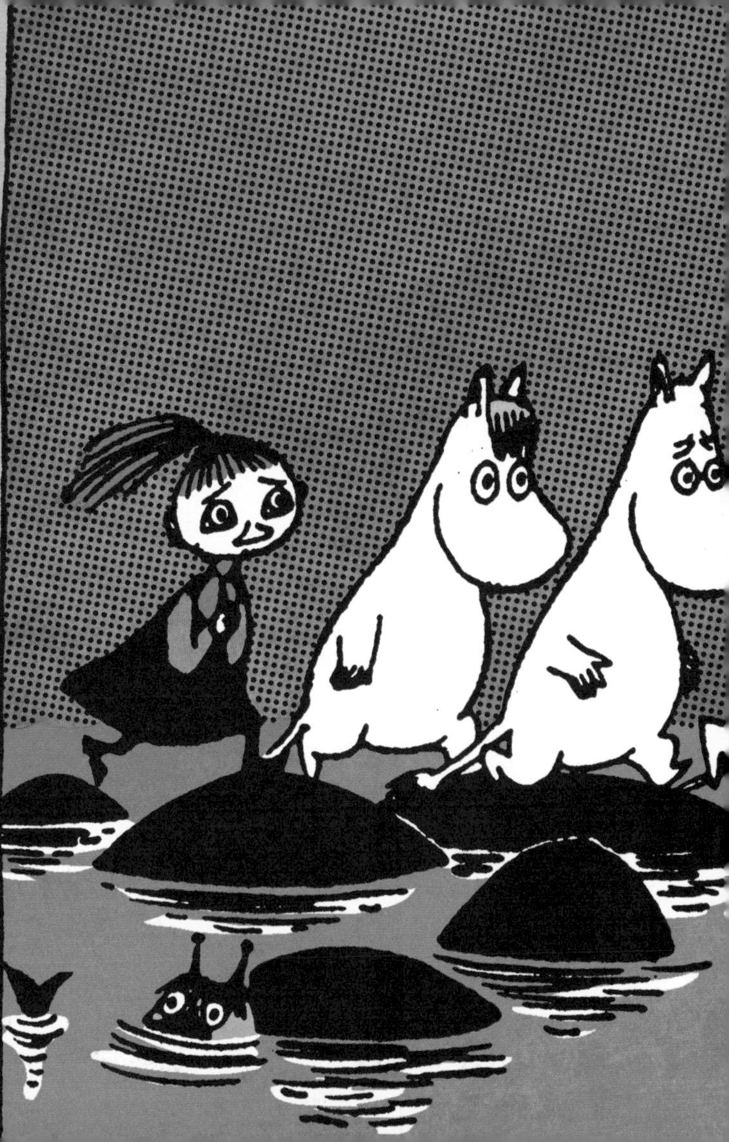

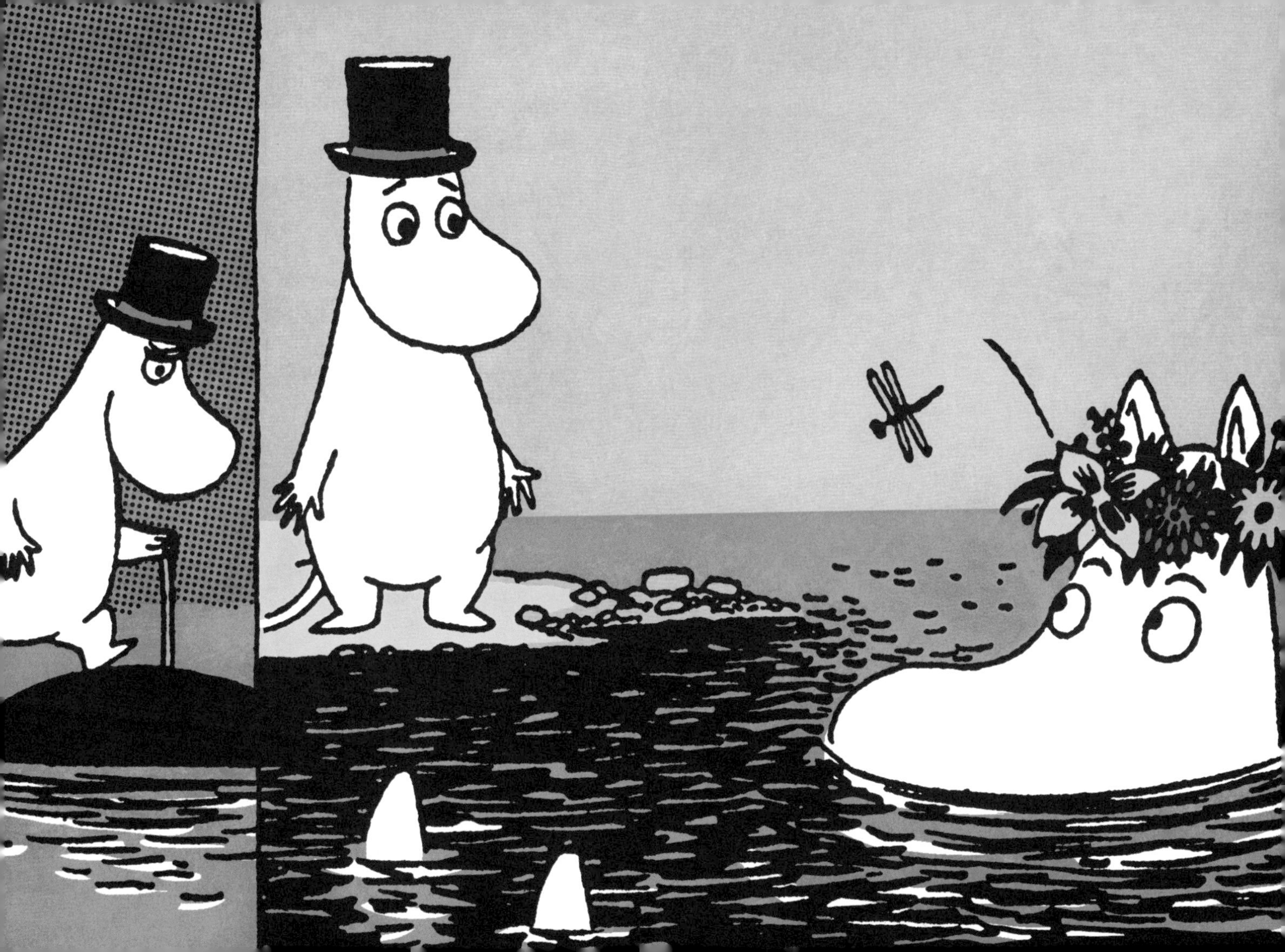

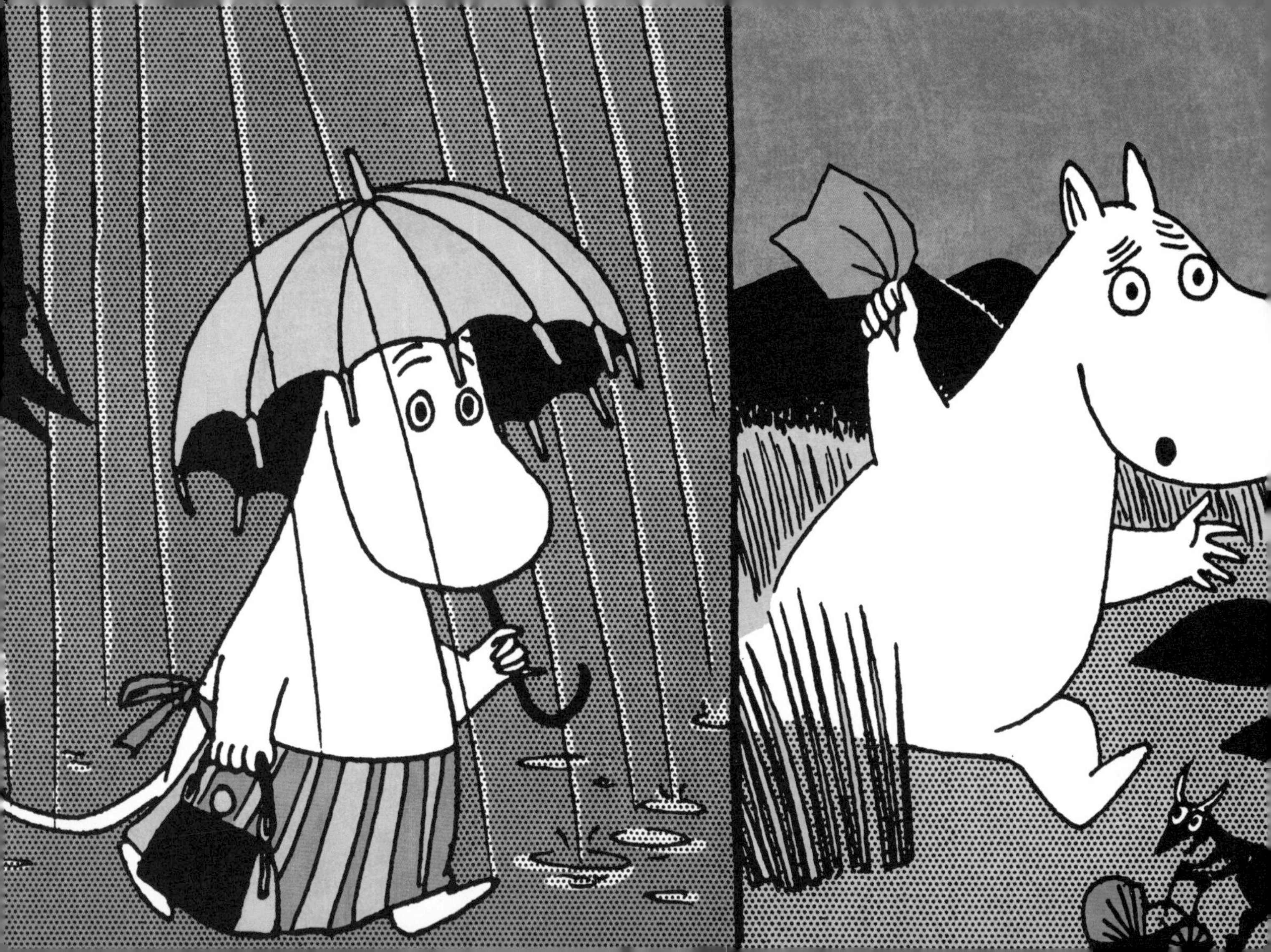

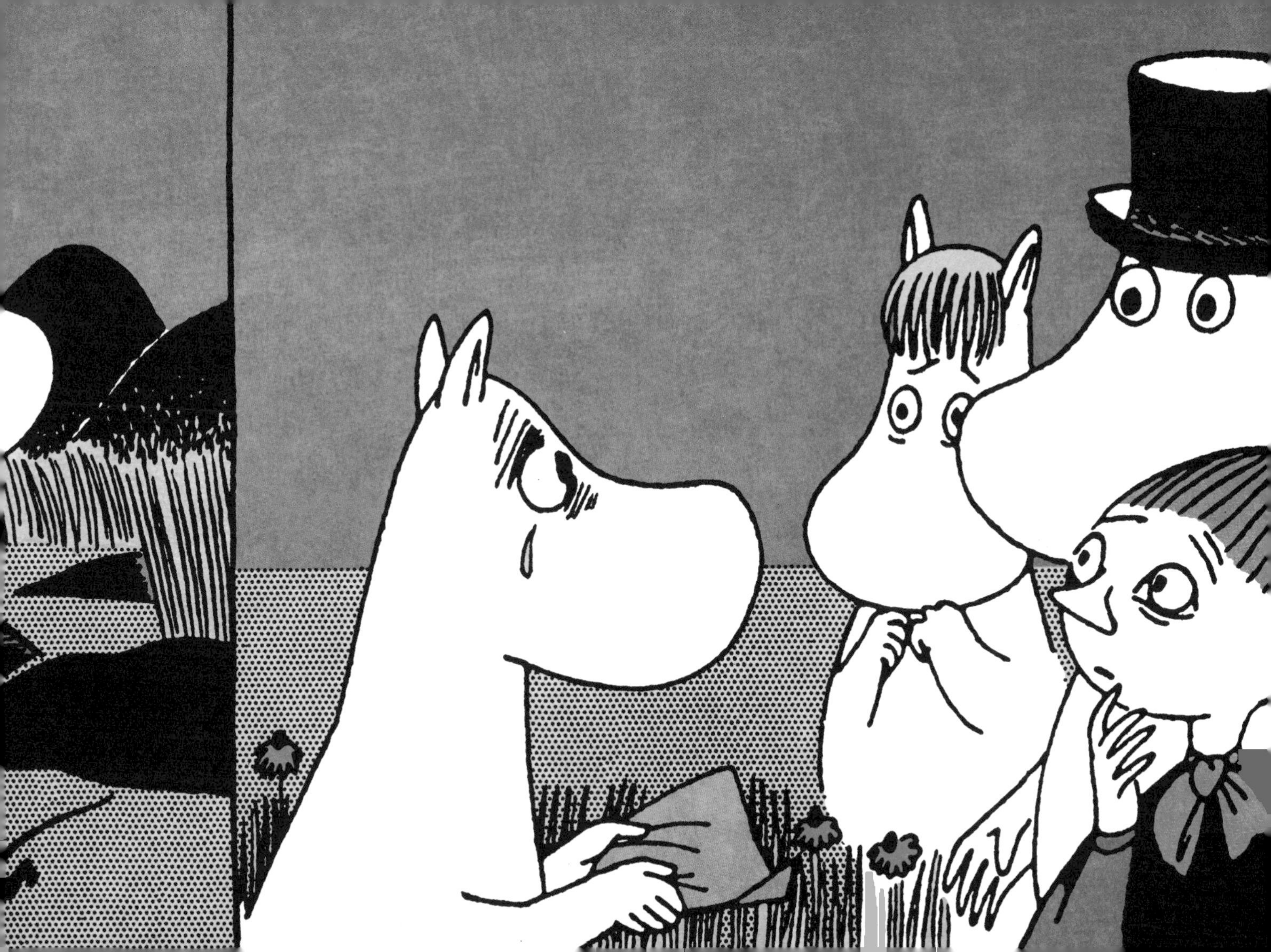

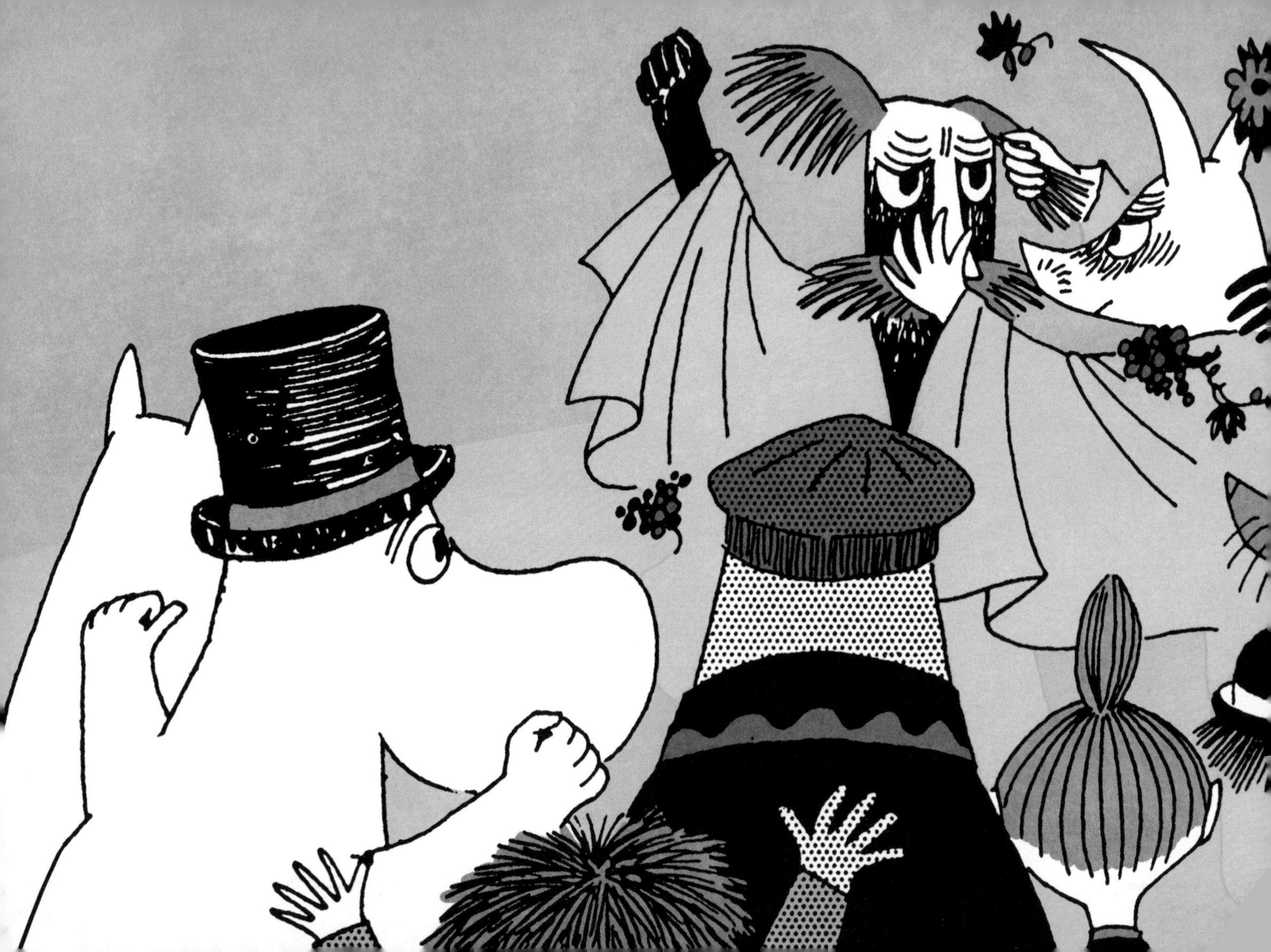